The Barefoot Book of
FAIRY TALES

To Sophia — *M. D.*

To Stefano with love and thanks — *N. C.*

Barefoot Books
2067 Massachusetts Ave
Cambridge, MA 02140

Text copyright © 2005 by Malachy Doyle
Illustrations copyright © 2005 by Nicoletta Ceccoli
The moral right of Malachy Doyle to be identified as the author
and Nicoletta Ceccoli to be identified as the illustrator of this work
has been asserted

This book has been printed on 100% acid-free paper

Graphic design by Katie Stephens, Bristol
Color separation by Bright Arts, Singapore
Printed and bound in China by South China Printing Co. Ltd

This book was typeset in 14pt Bembo and 35pt Medici Script
The illustrations were prepared in acrylics and pastels on Fabriano paper

1 3 5 7 9 8 6 4 2

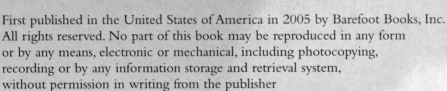

Library of Congress Cataloging-in-Publication Data

Doyle, Malachy.
  The Barefoot book of fairy tales / written by Malachy Doyle ; illustrated by Nicoletta
Ceccoli.
     p. cm.
  ISBN 1-84148-798-8 (hardcover : alk. paper)
  1. Fairy tales. [1. Fairy tales. 2. Folklore.] I. Ceccoli, Nicoletta, ill. II. Title.

PZ8.D7693Bar 2005
398.2—dc21

                            2004024657

The Barefoot Book of

FAIRY TALES

retold by Malachy Doyle

illustrated by Nicoletta Ceccoli

Barefoot Books
Celebrating Art and Story

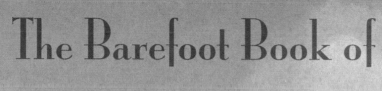

Contents

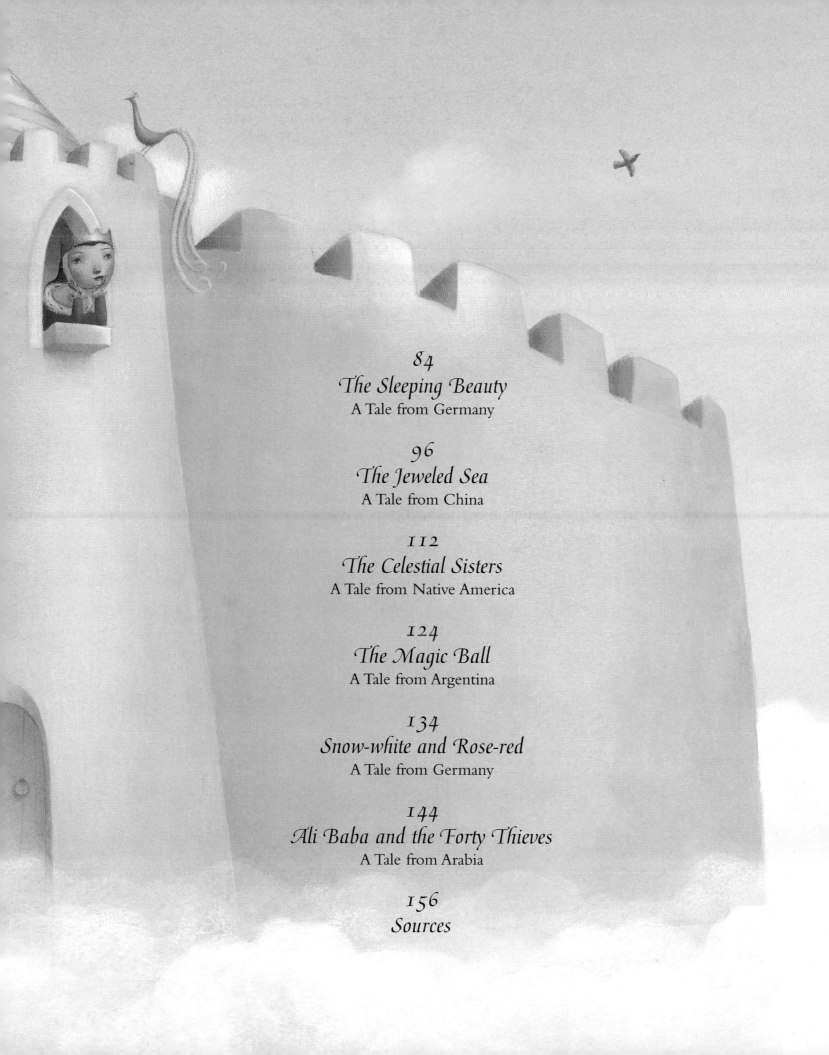

The Twelve Dancing Princesses

Long ago, in a land of mighty forests and rushing rivers, there was a king with twelve daughters. The beauty of the girls was famed far and wide, and all the young men in the land wished to marry them.

Every day a stream of suitors would arrive at the palace with flowers and cakes, poems and puppy dogs, but each time the king would take one look up and down the line and cry, "Clear off! You are not worthy of any one of my daughters!"

Fearing that the girls might meet and fall in love with the wrong sort of young men if they were allowed their freedom, the king made a rule that they were never allowed beyond the palace walls. And at night, as soon as they went to their room, he made sure that their door was firmly bolted.

But one morning, when his daughters came down for breakfast much later than usual, looking pale and tired, their father glanced down at their feet and noticed that their slippers were all worn out and broken.

"This will not do," he told the dressmaid. "I can't have my girls walking around like peasants. Run to the cobbler and fetch me another twelve pairs of the very best satin slippers."

And before the princesses had even finished their meal, twenty-four brand-new slippers had been produced.

The next morning, though, the slippers were in shreds yet again. "What have you been doing, girls?" the king asked. "How could you have worn them out so quickly?" But the princesses stared at their porridge, and not one of them would say a word.

The king asked the maid to run to the cobbler's and fetch twelve more pairs, but by the following morning they were worn out too. "You have been dancing, that's what you've been doing!" cried their father. "You have had strangers in your room, and you have been dancing all night!"

7

Their father took to watching outside their bedroom to see if anyone came or went, and listening at the door for the sound of tapping feet. But he never managed to stay awake long enough to find out what the girls were up to, and every morning, at breakfast, the slippers were as worn out as before.

The girls' secret and their lack of sleep were driving the king crazy, so he let it be known that if any man could find out what his daughters were doing in the night, he should be allowed to marry whichever princess he chose and inherit the kingdom. But he also announced that anyone wishing to attempt this had only three days and three nights in which to find out the answer to the problem, or he would be put to death.

"I should like to try, sir!" proclaimed the son of a lord, the first person to come forward.

"Fair enough," said the king, "but I hope you know what you're doing." He invited the young man to eat and drink with him, and then he brought him to the room next to the one in which the princesses slept. "Listen all night, then, and tell me in the morning what you've heard. But whatever you do, don't fall asleep!"

Try as he might, though, the son of a lord was soon snoring. And in the morning, when the princesses eventually made their way downstairs, the king inspected their slippers and he was furious.

"The soles, man, the soles!" he roared, holding a particularly worn-out pair right in front of the young man's face. "They're still full of holes!" But the son of a lord could offer no explanation.

The same thing happened the next night, and the next. The son of a lord was never able to stay awake long enough to find out what was going on, and so he faced the ultimate punishment. He was beheaded.

A few other reckless young men came to try their luck, but every one of them ended up the same way, and soon the word went around that, beautiful as the princesses were, they were not worth losing your head over.

One day, though, a soldier from a foreign land, who had been wounded in battle, found himself walking in the king's forest. He came upon an old woman, the two of them got talking, and soon enough he was told the whole story of the twelve beautiful princesses and their many, many slippers.

"So you say I could marry one of them and become king?" he asked.

"You could," replied the old woman, nodding. "If you do everything their father asks of you."

"Well, I think I'll give it a try," said the man. "For I've nothing to lose now that I can no longer earn my living as a soldier."

"I wish you luck, sir." The old woman bent down and reached into her bag. "My advice to you is to avoid anything the princesses give you to drink." She pulled out a brown and dusty cloak and handed it to him. "And to wear this at night, to make you invisible."

The soldier was not sure what to make of all this, but he went to the king and offered to watch over his daughters.

"You know that you have only three nights in which to find out their secret," the king warned him, surprised to see such a sensible-looking fellow willing to take such a risk.

"I know, my lord," answered the soldier and up he went, to the room next to the twelve princesses.

"Hello there, soldier," said one of the princesses, coming into his room with a goblet of wine. "Would you like a drink?"

"I would," replied the man. "Thank you." But when the girl's back was turned, he emptied the contents out of the window.

"Oh dear," he said, with a mighty yawn. "You must excuse me, ma'am, but I suddenly feel very tired. I think I'll just lie down for a minute." He staggered over to his bed, flung himself down upon it without even taking off his boots, and soon he began to snore.

"Hah!" cried the young princess, clapping her hands. "Another for the chopping block!" And she ran into the next room and told her sisters that they were safe.

The others laughed when they heard the news. Then they threw open their wardrobes and pulled out their finest ballgowns. They skipped about the room, admiring themselves, but the youngest was less happy than the others.

"I'm not so sure we should go tonight," she said. "I've a funny feeling there's something wrong."

"Oh, don't be so silly," replied her sister. "I've given that old soldier his medicine. He'll sleep like a horse!"

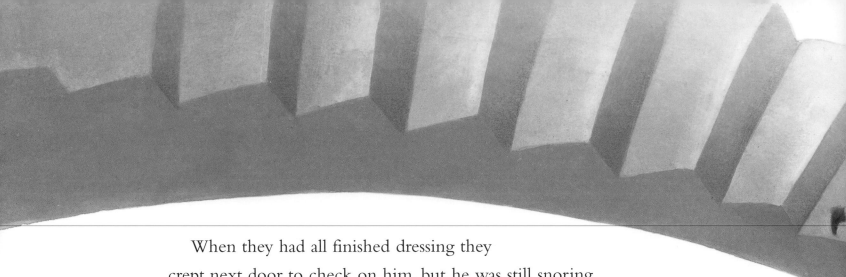

When they had all finished dressing they crept next door to check on him, but he was still snoring loudly, and even when they poked and tickled him, he did not stir. So they tiptoed back to their room. The eldest went over to the wall, tapped on it three times, and a magic door swung open. One after another, the princesses crept down the stairs on the other side, and off they went.

But the soldier, as we know, was only pretending to sleep. Throwing the cloak around his shoulders, he ran into the room just as the door was swinging shut. Squeezing through the gap, he followed the princesses down the stairs, but halfway down he slipped on the damp and darkened steps and almost crashed into the youngest one.

"Help! Help!" she cried, hearing the bashing and crashing. "There's someone behind me!"

"Oh, don't be so silly," said the eldest, up ahead. "It's just the sound of the door closing."

When they got to the bottom, they came into a line of trees, with the leaves all glittering like silver. The soldier, who knew he could not be seen, wanted to be able to prove to the king where he had been, so he snapped off a small branch.

"Help! Help!" yelled the youngest princess. "There's someone behind me! I'm sure I heard a noise."

"Don't be such a goose," the eldest mocked her. "It's only our princes, shouting for joy because they know we're on the way."

They raced down another line of trees, where the leaves were
all golden, and then a third, where they were glittering like
diamonds. Each time the soldier broke off a branch, and each time
the youngest princess nearly jumped out of her skin and
spun around to see what it was, but could see nothing.

On they went, until they came to a small lake,
and at the side of the lake were twelve
little boats. Inside each was a
handsome prince, and in next to
no time the princesses had
joined them and the twelve
little boats were sailing across
the lake. But, just in time, the
invisible soldier managed to
step into the boat with the
youngest princess, so as not to be
left behind.

"I must be tired tonight," said
her prince, as they fell behind the
others. "This boat feels strangely
heavy."

"It is a warm night," answered
the princess. "Maybe that is why
you are tired."

On the far side of the lake stood a wonderful castle. The princes tied up their boats, took their princesses by the hand, and led them up the steps and through the doors of the great hall. Inside, to the light of a thousand candles and the music of a hundred violins, they began to dance the night away. And the invisible soldier danced with them, taking care not to tread on anyone's toes.

By three in the morning, the slippers of the twelve dancing princesses were in shreds, and they had to stop dancing. The princes led them back down to the lake, rowed them across the water, and this time the soldier hid in the boat with the eldest sister, so that he was the first to land.

While the princes and princesses kissed each other good-bye and promised to meet up again the following night, he raced on ahead. Through the trees festooned with diamonds, gold and silver he ran, up the slippery stairs, through the magic door, which he had remembered

to leave slightly open, and into his bed. So that by the time the twelve princesses had limped home on their tired feet and broken slippers, he was snoring soundly, and this time it was for real.

The next morning, over a very late breakfast, the soldier did not say a word, even when the king asked him what he had discovered, and that night he followed the princesses again. Everything happened just as before, the beautiful girls danced the night away with their handsome princes until their brand-new satin slippers were falling apart, and then they returned home.

The same happened the third night, but this time the soldier carried away one of the golden goblets from the palace of the princes, as further proof of where he had been.

"So, soldier!" began the king, the following morning over breakfast. "The three nights are over, and you still haven't told me what my daughters have been up to."

At this, the soldier pushed back his chair, reached down under the table, pulled out the three branches and the golden cup, and held them up for everyone to see.

"What are you showing me, man?" asked the king. "What do this cup and these bits of wood have to do with my girls?"

"They come from a land under the ground," the soldier told him, "where your daughters go every night when you are asleep, my lord. They meet there with twelve princes and dance the night away!"

"Is this true?" cried the king, glowering at the princesses. "Have you been deceiving me all this time?"

"We had no choice, father. We were under a magic spell," said the eldest. "A spell which this handsome man," she added, smiling at the soldier, "has finally broken."

And with that, the twelve sisters rose from the table and made their weary way to their beds, where they slept for fourteen days and fourteen nights, to recover from their many nights of dancing.

"Thank you, kind sir," said the king to the soldier. "You have risked your life for me, and now I must repay you. You will be heir to my kingdom, and you may choose whichever of my daughters you would most like to marry."

The soldier waited until the sisters were well rested, and then he offered his hand to the eldest daughter, for she seemed the most sensible. She thanked him for breaking the mysterious enchantment they had been under, and agreed to marry him.

They had a magnificent wedding, to which all the young men of the land were invited, or all the ones the king approved of, anyway. And in next to no time every one of the twelve princesses had found themselves a kind and loving husband.

The Girl who Became a Fish

Once there was a girl who lived by the river, and all she ever wanted to do was to dance around the house or go out with her friends. Her mother and her father worked hard all day, but she never offered to help them, not once.

One day, though, something strange came over her. "Sit down, mother," she said. "You're looking very tired. Is there anything I can do to help?"

Her mother slumped into a chair, amazed to hear such kind words from her lazy daughter. "Well, yes, there is something, dear. Could you take your father's fishing net out and mend any holes you can see?"

So the girl did as she was asked. She bundled up the net in her arms, took it out to the river bank, found a comfortable place to sit and spent the morning mending holes until there was not a single one to be found.

She enjoyed herself, too, for everyone who went past, up and down the river on either side, stopped for a chat and to tell her how good it was to see her helping with the chores.

The girl was just folding the net to carry it back in when she heard a splash. Looking around, she saw a mighty fish jumping clear of the water. Quick as a flash, she spread the net wide and threw it out over the river.

Hauling it back in, she was delighted to see the fish thrashing about inside. "Got you!" she cried happily, for it was her first-ever catch. Then she looked more closely at the brightly colored fish. "Aren't you a beauty! Father will be proud of me."

But the fish stared back up at her with its sea-green eyes and replied, "You'd better not eat me, girl, for if you do, I'll turn you into a fish yourself!"

"Hah!" cried the girl, for she did not believe a word of it. Running straight to her mother, she led the old woman over to the river bank. "Come and see what I've caught! It's a talking fish, and it just told me that if I eat it, it'll turn me into a fish, too!" And she nearly doubled over with laughter.

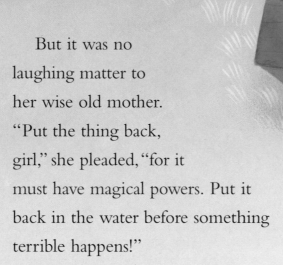

But it was no
laughing matter to
her wise old mother.
"Put the thing back,
girl," she pleaded, "for it
must have magical powers. Put it
back in the water before something
terrible happens!"

"Don't be silly, mother! We can't afford to
waste such a wonderful catch, and I'm so hungry, after
working hard all morning. Go and cook it, mother dear, and I'll be in
to eat it in a few minutes."

So the old woman, with a heavy heart, took the fish inside, and the
young girl ran off to gather flowers for her hair.

When she came back in, there was the fish, served up on a platter
in the middle of the table.

"It looks absolutely delicious!" cried the hungry girl, plunging her
fork into the dish and helping herself to a large piece. But as soon as it
touched her mouth, a cold shiver ran through her. Her head seemed
to flatten, her eyes began to dart all around, her arms and legs stuck to
her sides and she found herself gasping wildly for breath.

20

Then, spying the open window, she sprang through it with one great leap and landed with a splash in the cool, clear river.

Her horrified parents ran out after her, but all they could see was a shoal of fish, circling around in the water, and had no way of knowing which was their daughter. Her father rushed to fetch his net, but by the time he came back they had swum off, down toward the sea.

"What sort of fish are you?" asked the others, crowding around the shocked little fish-girl. "Where have you come from?"

"I'm not a fish at all," the newcomer spluttered, swallowing a load of water as she spoke. "I'm a girl. Or at least I was, until…" And she turned away, for she did not want them to see her crying.

"Until you caught a fish, I'd imagine," said a wise old haddock. "And you didn't believe it had the power to carry out its threat, did you? Well, never mind, the same thing happened to some of us here, and it's not such a bad life. Come along and meet our queen, for she lives in a beautiful palace."

So off they went, a great shoal of them, and the new little fish-girl was amazed at everything there was to see: jellyfish and multicolored seaweeds floating just below the surface, and further out and deeper, great sunken anchors, broken ships and treasures, so many treasures! Pearls and jewels and gold lay scattered about on the seabed and the bones of dead sailors poked up out of the sand.

"Here we are at last," cried the haddock, leading her into the palace.

The poor little fish-girl was exhausted from having swum so far and so fast, but she was struck by the beauty all around her. For the walls were made of pale pink coral, worn smooth by the waters, and around the windows were rows of pearls. The doors were standing open, and the whole troop floated into the great hall, where the queen, half woman, half fish, was seated on a throne of blue and green shell.

"Who have we here?" she asked, and the little fish-girl told her story.

"Now sit down here beside me," said the queen, when she had finished. "And I shall tell you my own story, for I also was once a girl. I married a prince and became queen of a faraway country. But a year later, when I was out in the garden with my baby son, a giant appeared and stole my crown. He told me he would give it to his daughter and enchant my husband so that he would think she was his wife, not me. I was so upset when I heard this that I threw myself into the sea, and my ladies-in-waiting, who loved me, followed me in. And here I must remain, until someone brings me back my crown."

"I will fetch it for you," cried the little fish-girl, for she was desperate to get back on dry land, whatever the cost.

"Do you think you could?" The queen studied her face. "First you must find the giant's castle, on the top of a high mountain, for I've heard that his daughter has since died, and the giant has the crown once more."

"I'll try," said the brave little fish-girl.

"Good luck, then. But you must be careful, for if the foul and horrible giant sees you, he will surely kill you. All I can give you, to help you in your quest, is the power to change into any animal you wish. Just strike your forehead and call out its name."

The next morning the fish-girl swam to shore, and when she got there she struck her forehead with her tail. "I want to be a deer!" she cried, and that moment she became a beautiful, proud beast, with branching horns and slender legs. Throwing back her head and sniffing the air, she broke into a run, leaping easily over the rivers, walls and hedges that stood in her way.

Now the king's son was out hunting and he spotted the deer. He raced after her on his swift-footed horse and soon caught up.

"Please do not kill me," the deer cried, pleading with her eyes, "for I have far to run and much to do."

The prince was amazed to hear a deer speak, and captivated by the beauty in her eyes. "This must surely be an enchanted maiden," he muttered to himself, as she raced free. "I will marry her and no other."

But the deer had gone and, try as he might, he could not find her.

When she arrived at the giant's castle, the walls were too high to jump. "I will be an ant!" she cried, and there and then she became a tiny insect, scuttling up the wall.

Soon she was over the top and down in the courtyard, where she spied a tall tree, reaching up to a high window. "And now I'll be a monkey," she whispered, and, in a second, a loose-limbed little monkey was swinging up through the branches and into the room where the giant lay snoring.

Then, "A parrot!" she cried, and flying on to

the giant's shoulder, she squawked in his ear, "The crown is no longer yours, big fellow, now that your daughter is dead!"

"What?" roared the giant, reaching out to grab the insolent bird.

"Spare me!" the parrot squawked. "Please spare me!"

"Why should I?" The giant tightened his grip. "Why should I take pity on a puny little parrot, who sneaks into my room, wakes me up by screeching into my ear, and tells me I have to give up my crown?" But then a thought slowly began to seep into his tiny brain, and he put down the frightened bird in order to scratch his head. "Not unless…you can bring me the thing I've always wanted. A collar of blue stones from the Arch of Saint Martin, in the Great City!"

"I'll do it straight away," said the parrot, hopping over to the window. She had no idea how she would manage it, but she was not going to tell the ugly great giant that.

"I want to be an eagle!" she cried and, quick as a flash, she became one, soaring high above the clouds.

Soon she was flying over the Great City. Spotting the famous arch, all set with beautiful stones, she swooped down and began to dig them out with her beak. It was hard work and painful, but eventually she had pried out enough to make a collar for the giant.

Stringing them on to a piece of string she had found hanging in a tree, she dangled it around her neck. "Now I want to be a parrot again!" And when she arrived back at the giant's castle, she flew up into his room and perched on his shoulder.

"Back already?" growled the big fellow. Then he noticed the collar of stones and, grabbing it, delighted, hung it around his bulgy neck.

"Now you must give me the crown, as we agreed," the parrot squawked, but the greedy giant had other ideas.

"They are not as blue as I thought," he complained, removing the necklace and holding the stones up to the light, pretending to be disappointed. "What I really want is a crown of stars from the sky. Go and bring me that instead."

The parrot was angry at being cheated, but she knew she was no match for the giant. "A toad! I will be a toad!" she cried, as soon as she had left the room, and sure enough she was one, hopping off in search of the stars.

She had not gone far when she came to a clear pool. Staring into the water, she saw the stars of the night sky, reflected so brightly that they looked real enough to hold. Scooping some up and popping them into her bag, she hopped back to the castle and made them into a crown.

"Here is your crown of stars," she squawked, having turned herself back into a parrot, and the ugly great giant cried out with wonder at their beauty.

"That's more like it!" he exclaimed in delight, crushing the crown on to his head. "Here, take the queen's crown, for this one is better by far."

The parrot seized it from the giant's hand and flew to the window. "Make me into a monkey!" she squawked, and she clambered down the tree that stood outside.

"Make me an ant!" And she crawled up and over the high wall.

Then, "A deer!" she squeaked and, as a fleet-footed deer, she raced over walls and rivers until she came to the sea.

"And now a fish!" she cried, plunging into the water and swimming to the beautiful underwater palace, where the queen and all the creatures of the sea were gathered together, waiting for her. But they had been waiting a long, long time, and some of them had quite given up hope of ever seeing her again.

"I'm tired of all this waiting," grumbled one. "I want to see what is happening up above. It must be months since that silly little fish-girl went away."

"I'd say the nasty giant's killed her, or she would have been back long ago," said another.

"The river flies will be out by now, and we will miss our chance to catch them," complained a third.

At that very moment a voice from behind them cried, "Look! Look at that sparkle of brightness, flashing toward us!" The crowd fell silent, and the queen rose up on her tail with excitement.

In came the little fish-girl, holding the crown tightly in her mouth, and all of the other sea creatures moved aside to let her pass. On she swam, right to the mermaid queen, who took hold of the beautiful crown and placed it on her head.

And then a wonderful thing happened. The queen's tail turned into legs, and her handmaidens, all around her, shed their scales and became girls again. They stood around, admiring one another and then admiring the little fish, who had regained her own shape and was more beautiful than any of them.

"You have given us back our life!" they cried, crowding around her and weeping for joy.

They soon said farewell to the creatures of the sea and returned to land. The queen was thrilled to see her husband again, and particularly pleased to see her son, for she had left when he was only a babe in arms. But there was an air of sadness about the young man, even though his mother had returned at last.

"What's wrong, my dear?" she asked him, as they walked together in the garden. "If I can give you happiness, it will be yours."

"No one can," said the prince, sadly. "For I have fallen in love with someone I can never marry, and I must carry my sadness alone." And he told her about the deer in the forest, and how he had fallen head over heels in love with her as soon as he looked into her eyes.

"Ah!" said the queen, with a smile. "I think I know how to help you." For she knew, right away, that it was the fisherman's daughter that her son had encountered.

She called for the girl, who had not yet returned home to her parents, and when the prince saw her he was struck dumb by the beauty of her.

The young woman came closer, and her eyes were those of the deer in the forest. "Please do not kill me," she whispered in the prince's ear, "for I have far to run and much to do."

"The very words you used when we met in the forest! I have found you at last, my love!" The young man took her in his arms, and their hearts were filled with joy.

And the queen, his mother, watched them and smiled.

Hansel and Gretel

"What's to become of us?" said a poor woodcutter to his wife one evening. "How can we feed the children when there isn't even enough for ourselves?"

"Sssh, man." His wife pointed to the wall. "Sssh, and I'll tell you." And she dropped her voice to a whisper, for fear that little Hansel and Gretel, asleep in the next room, might hear. "Tomorrow morning we'll take them deep into the forest. We'll give them some bread, to take away the worst of their hunger, and we'll leave them there."

"What?" cried her husband. "We can't just abandon them in the forest! They'll freeze to death! Wild animals will tear them to pieces!"

"Keep your voice down," hissed his wife. "There's no food left! If we don't do something, every one of us will die."

The poor woodcutter was silent then. "If they were her own children, she wouldn't dream of such a thing," he muttered under his breath, for Hansel and Gretel's real mother had died some years before, and his new wife did not love the two children as their father would have wished.

But she was a strong-minded woman, and he did not dare to argue with her. In addition, he knew that in some ways she was right — there was hardly a scrap of food left to eat, and if he did not do something he might as well go out and make four wooden coffins, one for each of the family.

"All right," he said to his wife at last, silent tears slipping down his face. "We will do as you say."

But Hansel and Gretel were not asleep. They were lying awake in the next room, their stomachs heavy with hunger, and they heard every word their parents spoke.

"It's the end of us," cried the poor little girl, sobbing bitterly.

"Don't weep, Gretel," whispered her brother. "I'll look after you." And he lay awake, racking his brain to think of a way to save them.

When Hansel heard their parents snoring at last, he slipped out of bed, threw on his coat and crept outside. The full moon was shining brightly and the little white pebbles that lay all around the house glittered like silver. Bending down, he filled his pockets with them and then went back to bed.

Early the next morning, before the sun was up, the woodcutter's wife came and woke the two children. "Get up, you lazybones! We're off to the forest to gather wood."

"So early?" said Hansel, turning over in his bed. But his stepmother tore back the cover and left him there, shivering.

When they were ready to go out, she gave each child a small piece of bread. "Don't eat it now," she warned. "It's all you've got to last the day, so make sure you keep it till you're really hungry."

Hansel slipped his to Gretel, as his pockets were already full of stones, and off they went, into the deep, dark forest.

"Hurry up, Hansel!" the woman screeched, for the boy kept falling behind. "See…" she whispered to her husband, "we're doing him a kindness. He can't even keep up with his own sister anymore."

But Hansel was a clever fellow, and what he had been doing was laying a line of shiny white pebbles along the path, so that he and Gretel would be able to find their way back home.

When they got to a clearing, deep in the heart of the forest, their father said, "Find some wood, children, and I'll make us a fire so we don't freeze."

"Don't be silly, man," his wife sneered. "We're supposed to be collecting it, not burning it."

But their father insisted, so Hansel and Gretel gathered sticks and made a pile in the clearing. "More! We need more!" the woodcutter cried. His wife gave him a strange look, but she did not say anything, and the children went off again.

When the pile of brushwood was a decent size, their father lit the fire. And when the flames were leaping high, the woman rubbed her hands together and said, "That's a lovely fire, children. You must be tired, with all your hard work. Why not sit down and have a rest, while your father and I go into the forest to chop wood? We'll be back to fetch you when we're done."

Hansel and Gretel curled up by the fire, and when midday came
the young girl took the bread from her pocket and shared it between
them. "Have they gone home without us, Hansel?"

"I don't think so," the boy answered. "For I can still hear the
sound of father's ax."

But it was only a trick, for when their stepmother had left
the clearing, she had tied a branch to a dead tree, and the
sound of the two knocking against each other in the
wind was just like the blows of an ax.

The fire was warm and the children were tired,
so they curled up against each other again and
soon fell asleep. And when they woke up, the
fire was out, the last of the light was gone
from the day and there was no sign of
their parents, not anywhere.

"What will we do?" asked Gretel,
starting to cry.

But Hansel put his arm around
her. "Don't worry, sister. Just wait
until the moon comes up and I'll
find our way home."

Sure enough, as soon as it
rose high enough in the sky
for its light to shine down
between the trees, Hansel led
her to the edge of the
clearing. "Look," he said,
showing her a bright little

33

pebble shining on the path. "All we have to do is follow these and we'll be safe and sound." And that is what they did.

It was early the next morning by the time they got back to their parents' house. It was all locked up, so Hansel had to rap on the door.

"You wicked children!" cried their stepmother, shocked to see them. "What were you thinking of, staying out all night?"

But their father was delighted to have them back. He held them tightly and vowed, under his breath, never to be so cruel again.

The family managed to find enough food to survive the next few months, but winter brought hard times, even harder than before.

"Those children are eating us out of house and home, husband," hissed his wife one night. "There's half a loaf of bread left, and that's it."

"What do you suggest?" asked the man, with a heavy heart.

"There's only one thing for it. We must take them even deeper into the forest, and this time we must make sure they don't come back!"

The woodcutter could not bear it, but he did not have the courage to stand up to her, and so he said nothing. Once again, though, the children were lying awake, and they heard every word. So Hansel waited until his parents were asleep, jumped out of bed and ran down to gather up the white pebbles, as he had done before. But his stepmother had guessed his little secret and had taken to locking the doors and windows and hiding the key, so there was no way out.

"I couldn't find any pebbles," he told his sister, when he returned to their room. "But don't cry, Gretel. I'll think of something."

Early the next morning, their stepmother hauled them out of bed. She gave them each a piece of bread, even smaller than before, and this time it was Hansel who whispered to his sister, "Let me carry your bread, Gretel. I'll keep it safe."

But all along the way into the deep, dark forest, he sprinkled tiny crumbs of bread on the path, so he would be able to find the way back.

"Get a move on, boy!" the woman hollered, annoyed that Hansel was falling behind again. But she nudged her husband and whispered, "The poor lad's even weaker than before, and his sister's not much better. We'll only be putting them out of their misery."

On and on they went, deeper and deeper into the forest, until even the woodcutter was not too sure of the way back. "We'd better not go any farther," he warned, and he set them to building a fire, just as he had before.

"Stay here where it's warm, children," their stepmother told them, "and if you feel tired, you can sleep for a while. Your father and I are just going into the forest to chop wood. We'll come and fetch you when we're done."

There was no bread to share this time, for all of it lay scattered on the path behind them, so the children curled up by the fire, tired and hungry, and soon they were fast asleep.

No one came to fetch them, of course, and when they woke it was cold and dark and the fire was out. "Don't be afraid, Gretel," said Hansel, trying to comfort her. "Just wait till the moon's high in the sky and we'll be able to see all the tiny scraps of bread I've dropped and follow them home."

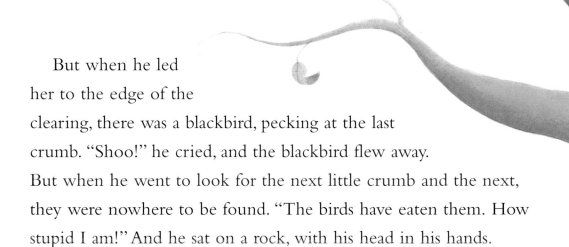

But when he led
her to the edge of the
clearing, there was a blackbird, pecking at the last
crumb. "Shoo!" he cried, and the blackbird flew away.
But when he went to look for the next little crumb and the next,
they were nowhere to be found. "The birds have eaten them. How
stupid I am!" And he sat on a rock, with his head in his hands.

They walked and they wandered, all through the forest, but every
path they followed ended in disappointment. All night long they tried
to find the way, and all the next day too, until they were nearly
dropping to the ground with tiredness and hunger. The only things
they found to eat were a few wild berries, and when they were so
tired that their legs would not carry them a single step farther, they lay
on the ground and they slept.

They woke to the sound of birdsong. A beautiful little bird, as blue
as the sky, was sitting on a branch close by, singing the sweetest song
they had ever heard. They watched, without speaking, and when the
bird flew off, they felt drawn to follow it.

It led them through the trees and into a clearing, and there in front
of them was the prettiest cottage. The children laughed at the sight of
it, for surely such a sweet little house could only belong to a kind

37

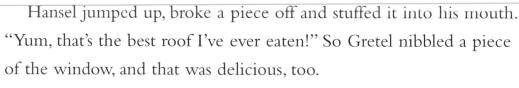

person, and surely that meant that their troubles were over. They rushed forward into the clearing and then stopped in amazement, for the walls were made of gingerbread, the roof was cake and the windows were nothing but sugar.

Hansel jumped up, broke a piece off and stuffed it into his mouth. "Yum, that's the best roof I've ever eaten!" So Gretel nibbled a piece of the window, and that was delicious, too.

Just then a thin little voice came from inside:

"*Nibble, nibble, little mouse,*

Who's eating my house?"

But the children were so delighted with the wonderful food that they did not even notice. Hansel tugged at the roof, till the corner fell off, and Gretel shoved a whole windowpane into her mouth.

The front door opened and out came an old woman, leaning on a stick. "Ah," she said, licking her lips, "two sweet little, lost little, hungry little children! Come inside and I will take very good care of you."

She took them each by the hand and led them into the house, where she prepared the most delicious dinner — milk and pancakes, apples and nuts. And when they had filled their stomachs, she made up cozy little beds by the fire, and Hansel and Gretel settled down to sleep.

But the old woman was in fact an evil witch, and the only reason she had built a gingerbread house was to entice young children into her lair. So early the next morning she dragged young Hansel from his bed and took him to a shed, where she locked him in. "Scream as much as you like, boy," she cackled. "It won't do you any good."

Then she shook little Gretel awake. "Get up, you lazybones," she screeched, "and cook some food for your brother, for I'm going to fatten him up and eat him!" Poor Gretel cried and cried, but she did as the witch said, for she knew she had no choice.

So young Hansel got the best of everything while his sister got nothing but crab shells. Every morning the wicked old witch would hobble down to the shed and shriek, "Poke out your finger, boy, and I'll see if you're fat enough to eat yet!"

But Hansel still had his wits about him. He picked up a thin little bone, left over from the soup he had had the night before, and poked it through the gap in the door. The old witch, who could not see very well, took hold of it and cried, "What's the matter, boy? Is the food not good enough for you?" And, disgusted with how thin he still was, she went back and got Gretel to cook up something even better.

Now this went on, day after day, and when four whole weeks had passed and Hansel still did not seem to be getting any fatter, the old witch finally lost her patience.

"That's it, Gretel! I'm fed up waiting for that stupid brother of yours to put on weight. Fetch a big pan of water for I'm going to cook him tomorrow morning, whether he's plump or skinny!"

Gretel bawled her eyes out at the thought of her poor brother being boiled in the pan. "If only the wild beasts in the forest had eaten us, at least we'd have died together," she lamented.

"Ah, spare me your weeping and wailing, girl! For what will happen will happen, and there's not a thing you can do to change it."

So early the next morning, poor Gretel dragged herself out of bed, hung up the big cauldron and lit the fire.

"First we'll do some baking," cackled the witch. "I've already heated the oven and kneaded the dough." And she led little Gretel to the oven. "You go inside and check it's warming properly, and then we'll slide in the bread." What she really had in mind, of course, was to lock the door on her and make a meal of poor Gretel, too.

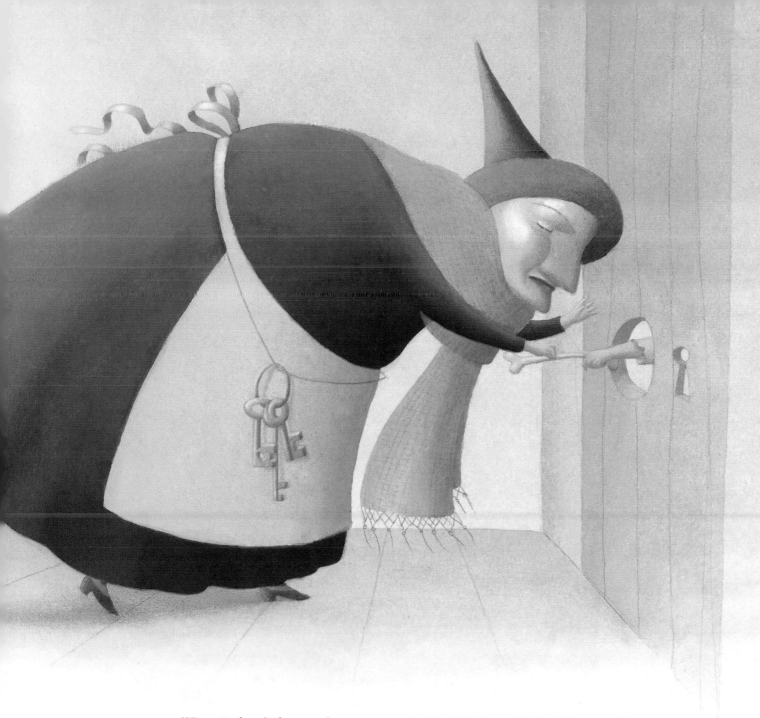

"But I don't know how to get in," said the girl, looking at the great red flames pouring out from all sides and thinking there was no way she was going in there. "You'd better show me how, for I don't think it's big enough."

"You stupid goose," screamed the witch. "Of course it's big enough. Look, even I could get in!" And she bent over and stuck her head in the oven, to show the girl what to do.

Then Gretel gave her a mighty shove, slammed shut the great iron door and off she ran. What a howling there was from inside! But Gretel was already on her way to the shed. "She's dead! She's dead!" she yelled, throwing open the door and hugging her brother. "I shoved her in the oven and baked her alive!"

"Well done, little sister!" cried Hansel, and they raced back into the witch's house and gathered up all the gold and silver they could find. Then they ran and they ran, with the sound of the witch's screams still ringing in their ears, and this time they had no problem finding their way home. When they arrived, their father hugged them and kissed them and said what a terrible thing he had done, leaving them in the forest. He told them that he had gone back, every day, to look for them, but he had never been able to find them.

"What about our stepmother?" asked Hansel, looking around nervously. "Where is she?"

"I'm afraid she's gone," said their father. And he told them that his wife had died from lack of food and that he had nearly died himself, from a broken heart at the loss of his beloved children. "But now you're back, my darlings, I shall be a good father from this day on."

Hansel and Gretel gave him the gold and the silver they had brought from the witch's house, their father was even more delighted, and they were rich enough to never be hungry again.

Cinderella

This is the story of poor little Ella. She lived far away, in a time long ago, and she was the hardest-working girl in the land, for she never got a moment's peace.

"Clean the dishes, girl!"

"Yes, mother."

"Sweep the floor, girl!"

"Yes, mother."

"Make the beds and fetch the water, light the fire and cook us some food, girl!"

"Yes, mother. Of course, mother."

But it was not Ella's real mother ordering her about. Her real mother had died when Ella was young, and in time her father had married again. His new wife, and the two daughters that the grumpy woman had brought with her, were the most unpleasant people you were ever likely to meet. They stayed in bed until late in the morning, they were lazy as lazy could be, they expected poor Ella to do all the work around the house and they never had a single kind word or thought for her, not once.

"Tidy my room!"

"Cut my toenails!"

"Sweep out the cinders and bring us some food!"

And that is what they called her — Cinderella. For not only had she to clear out the cinders from the corner by the fire, but she had to sleep there, too.

One day word came that the king's son was to have a ball — a wonderful party of music and dancing. The whole household was invited, and the two sisters were almost out of their minds with excitement.

"I shall dance with the prince," vowed the dumpy one, "and he will fall head over heels in love with me!"

"No, he shall dance with me and no one else!" insisted the lumpy one. "And at the end of the evening he will get down on bended knee and ask me to be his wife."

And they spent all day, every day, for the next two weeks, preening and fussing and choosing their clothes.

"Iron my dress, girl!"

"Polish my shoes!"

"Sew up my hem!"

"Just make me look beautiful!"

So poor little Cinderella had to spend all day, every day, running around after them and doing everything she could to turn her lumpy, dumpy sisters into creatures of beauty.

"I suppose you're upset, little Cinders," smirked the lumpy one, admiring herself in the looking glass while her hair was being combed, "because you can't come with us."

"I would dearly love to go," answered the girl, for she only ever told the truth, "but there is too much work to do here."

"There certainly is!" roared the other one. "And what a laughing-stock we'd be if we brought scrubby little Cinders with us, in all her dust and her dirt!" And that was that. No more was said about it.

On the evening of the ball, Cinderella dressed them in their finery, pinned up their hair and did all in her power to make her sisters as attractive as possible. It was only when they had gone off in their coach and the house was empty that the poor girl broke down and cried.

"If only… If only…"

And suddenly, much to Cinderella's amazement, there by her side was her fairy godmother.

"What would you wish for, my kindhearted girl?" asked the funny little woman with stars on her head and a wand in her hand.

"I'd wish…" began Cinderella. "Oh, I'd wish…"

"To go to the ball!" cried the fairy. "Wouldn't you?"

And Cinderella nodded, shyly.

"Well, why shouldn't you?" declared the fairy. "It's not right, the way that stepmother of yours and her two daughters never let you go anywhere. For you're a kinder, sweeter, prettier girl than either of them will ever be! Now go and fetch me a pumpkin, love, and we'll see what we can do about it."

So Cinderella went out into the garden and pulled up the largest pumpkin she could find, though she had no idea how it might help her get to the ball. Her fairy godmother scooped out all the insides, leaving nothing but the rind. Then she struck it with her magic wand, and instantly it turned into the finest golden coach, all lined inside with rose-colored satin.

"Are there any mice in the house?" the little woman asked, and Cinderella went to check the grain cupboard,

where she found six squeaky mice.

She somehow managed to bundle them all up and
brought them to her fairy godmother, who tapped each one with
her wand, and there and then they became six fine horses.

"Have you a rat, by any chance?" she asked, and Cinderella went
down to the cellars and came back with a fat, squeaky rat, dangling by
its tail. Tappity tap, and it became a jolly coachman, with the smartest
whiskers you have ever seen.

"Now go and look under the watering can," said the fairy godmother, "and see what you can find." And when Cinderella went to look, there were six slippery lizards, which the magical woman turned in an instant into a batch of handsome footmen.

"Now in you hop, and you're off to the ball!" she told the girl.

"Oh, thank you!" cried Cinders, looking all around. "Everything is so beautiful." But then she looked down at the rags she stood up in. "Everything, that is, except me."

"Oh, but you ARE beautiful!" declared the fairy woman, tapping her with the wand. "And I shall give you clothes to match your beauty. For you are the kindest, sweetest, most radiant girl in all the land, and if the king's son doesn't agree, then he's a frog."

Instantly, Cinderella's clothes turned to gold and to silver, a shimmer of lace and a sparkle of jewels. She looked at her feet and gasped, for her legs were clothed in the finest of silk, and her slippers were glass and as pretty as pearls.

"Now, Cinderella, you may go to the ball. But there are two things that I need you to promise me, child," said her godmother, kissing her on the cheek. "One is to have a wonderful, wonderful time…"

"And the other?" Cinderella beamed.

"The other is to make certain that you're gone from the palace before midnight, or the magic will fail and all may be lost!"

Cinderella promised, and then up she popped, into the coach, and off the six fine horses trotted to the ball.

"Who can it be?" asked everyone, when they saw such a magnificent coach and horses approaching.

"Oh, who on earth can it be?" they
repeated, when Cinderella stepped down
from the coach in all of her beauty.

The dancing stopped, as even the
musicians put down their instruments in order
to get a good look at the mysterious stranger,
making her fabulous entrance. The king's son
came to see what all the fuss was about, and when
he beheld Cinderella in all her loveliness, there was
nothing for it but for him to dance with her all night.

Cinderella had the most wonderful evening she had ever
had in her whole life, but time flashed by in the blink of an eye, and
just before the chimes of midnight, she suddenly remembered her
fairy godmother's warning. Slipping from the prince's grasp, she ran to
her coach and away.

Changing back into her rags as soon as she got home, she was
sitting in the corner by the fire, rubbing her eyes and pretending to be
exhausted with all the hard work she had had to do around the house,
when in strode her two sisters.

"You wouldn't believe what an amazing time we had at the ball!"
cried the lumpy one. "Everyone who is anyone was there!"

"And you'll never guess, but the king's son has declared that there'll
be another ball tomorrow night!" announced the dumpy one. "And
we're invited to that one as well!" And they yawned their way to bed,
dropping their clothes all around them as they went. For it was not
they who would have to pick them up and wash and iron them, of
course. It was poor little Cinders.

The king's son, you see, was head over heels in love with the
mysterious stranger. He was frantic when she slipped away without

even telling him her name, so he let it be known, there and then, that there would be another ball the very next night, in the hope that she would return.

Cinderella had to spend the whole of the following day doing her level best to make her ungrateful sisters worthy of the prince's attention. But when she had finally packed them off to the ball, her fairy godmother appeared once more and gave her everything she required in order to make an even more spectacular entrance.

The king's son was waiting on the drive for her coach to arrive. He offered his hand to help her down, and would not let go of it all night.

They had such a wonderful time together, dancing the night away, for by now Cinderella loved the handsome prince just as much as he loved her.

But she was so caught up in the excitement of it all that she forgot to keep an eye on the time, and it was only when she heard the first chime of midnight filling the room that she remembered what her fairy godmother had told her.

Slipping from the prince's grasp, she sprinted back to her coach, but she ran so fast that she tripped on the steps, losing one of the glass slippers as she fell. Picking herself up, Cinderella made a dash for the coach but, just as she got there, the last chime of midnight struck and there and then the coach became a pumpkin, the horses mice, the coachman a rat, the footmen lizards, and her clothes nothing but rags.

With a gasp of horror, Cinderella slipped away into the darkness. Then she ran all the way home, to make sure she arrived back before her sisters, and she was weary and breathless, ragged and cold by the time she got there. All she had left to remind her of the wondrous night was one little glass slipper which, for some strange reason, had not disappeared when the magic came undone.

"How was the ball?" she asked her sisters, when they returned.

"It was superb!" said the first. "The prince even smiled at me."

"Oh, he'd a smile three times round his face, all right," said the second, with a sneer. "But it wasn't at you he was smiling, you silly goose. It was only because he was in the arms of that woman again!"

"Which woman?" asked Cinderella, innocently.

"Oh, the one who was there last time. Some princess from a foreign land. No one knows who she is, but she's won his heart all right. I was trying to catch his eye all evening, and he looked straight through me."

"Oyez! Oyez!" It was early the next morning, and the royal messenger was out ringing his bell, all around town. "The king's son

has found a glass slipper and has vowed to marry the woman whose foot it fits!"

The lumpy, dumpy sisters and their grumpy mother jumped out of bed and ran to join the line of people trying on the little glass slipper that Cinderella had lost. But, no matter how hard they tried, they could not convince the prince that the slipper was theirs, for it was far too small for them and their bunions.

"Maybe it might fit me," suggested young Cinderella, hurrying out to join them.

"Don't be ridiculous!" hissed her sisters, furious at their rejection. "That slipper belongs to the magnificent princess from the ball, not some scabby little ash-girl! Get back in and finish your chores, girl, and don't embarrass us, out here in front of the prince!"

But the king's son heard their unpleasantness, and he gave them a fierce look. "Everyone may try!" he declared, beckoning Cinderella forward. So she sat herself down in front of him and gently he placed the slipper on her foot. And would you believe it, but it fit her like a glove!

"But how…?" gasped the king's son, looking her up and down in her tatters and rags. "How could you be my wondrous beauty?"

And at that, Cinderella pulled the second glass slipper from the pocket of her raggedy dress and placed it on her other foot. As her sisters gasped in horror, the fairy godmother appeared out of nowhere and tapped Cinderella on the shoulder with her wand. Instantly the little ash-girl was in the finest of clothes, and everyone could tell that she was the most radiant, sparkling beauty they had ever seen.

The prince took her by the hand and proceeded to waltz her around the lawn. "Marry me!" he declared, when they came to a dizzy halt. "For now that I have found you, my love, I cannot bear to let you go until you agree to be my wife."

Cinderella smiled up at him and said she would, and they were married that very day. She allowed her jealous sisters to be her bridesmaids, her astonished stepmother to carry her train, her proud father to walk her up the aisle, and now she is the queen of all the land.

The Fool of the World
and the Flying Ship

A long time ago, in a small country town, there lived a man and a woman and their three healthy sons. The two elder boys were as bright as buttons, but the third was a complete and utter dunce, or at least that is what everyone thought.

One day, word reached the town that the king had offered his only daughter in marriage to anyone who would come to his court with a ship that could fly.

"A flying ship!" cried the father. "What a strange idea!"

"Oh, not so strange," said the first brother. "I'm sure I could make one, if I set my mind to it."

"Not strange at all," said the second. "I'm sure I could make one, too."

"What clever young men you both are!" declared their mother, and she gave each boy a new set of clothes, some food for the journey, and off they went to the court of the king, to make a ship that could fly and win the hand of a princess.

"What about me, mother?" asked the third brother, when the other two had gone.

"You?" the woman laughed.

"Yes, me," said young Erik. "I don't see why I shouldn't get a new set of clothes and a chance to make my fortune, too."

"Hah!" cried his mother. "What chance would you have of marrying a princess? They'd laugh you out of court as soon as look at you!"

"They wouldn't."

"They would."

"They wouldn't."

"They would."

Poor Erik insisted that he should at least be given a chance, so his mother found him a crust of bread and a bottle of water and off he went, with nothing but that, the clothes on his back and an ax.

Well, he hadn't gone far when he met a manikin, sitting on a wall.

"Hello, little man," said Erik.

"Hello there," replied the manikin, in a squeaky voice. "And where are you off to, this fine summer morning?"

"I'm off to the king's court," answered Erik. "He's promised to give his only daughter in marriage to the first person who can make him a flying ship."

"A flying ship!" said the little man. "And can you do such a thing?"

"I shouldn't think so," said the boy, downcast.

"Then why in the world are you going?"

"I don't really know, to tell you the truth," answered Erik. "But my two clever brothers went there before me, and I didn't want to be left at home, twiddling my thumbs."

"Sit down here and we'll have a think about it." The manikin patted the wall beside him. "But before we get down to all that, I could do with something to eat. Have you anything good in that bag of yours?"

Erik was ashamed to open it up, for he knew all he had was a crust of bread and a bottle of water, but he was a kind and gentle boy, and he felt it was right to share whatever he had. Wasn't he amazed, though, when he opened the bag, to find two fresh rolls and the very best of meat!

They shared their
food and the manikin was
delighted. "Now I'll tell you what to
do, young fellow. You're to go into that wood
over there, stop in front of the first tree you come to,
bow three times, strike it with your ax and fall to the
ground, asleep."

"And why would I want to do that?" asked Erik, frowning.

"Because when you wake up, you'll see a ship at your side. A ship
that can fly better than any bird you've ever seen! You're to climb in
and fly to the king's palace. But if you notice anyone on the way, be
sure to stop and take him with you. Will you remember all that?"

"I'll do my best," said the boy, not really believing for a minute that
such an amazing thing was likely to happen. "And thank you for your
advice, sir."

"No, it's you that should be thanked, young man. For seventeen people went past me today before you came along, and not a single one even said hello, never mind offered to share their food."

Erik said good-bye, and he went over the road to the wood, where he did exactly as he had been told. He bowed three times to the first tree he saw, struck it with his ax and fell to the ground, asleep.

And wasn't he amazed when he woke to see a ship, a whole ship, at his side! He blinked and rubbed his eyes, but it was really there, just as the little man had said it would be. So he climbed up into it and, as soon as he did so, the ship took off, into the air.

Well, Erik was beside himself with joy, but he was wise enough to remember the other thing the manikin had told him, and that was to keep a lookout over the side, in case he should see anyone.

He soared over mountains and forests and lakes, and there was not a single person below, but at last he saw a man beneath him, with his ear to the ground.

"What are you doing, sir?" cried the boy.

The man looked up and did not seem the slightest bit surprised to see a flying ship above him. "I'm listening to what's going on in the world," said he.

"That's odd," thought Erik, but by this time he was getting used to odd things happening, so he invited the man to join him. "Come with me in my ship," he offered, "and you'll not only be able to hear what's happening in the world, but you'll be able to see it as well."

"I will, and thank you." The man grabbed the rope the boy threw down, climbed up, and off they went.

They flew and they flew till they saw another man, hopping along, with one leg tied behind him.

"Why are you hopping?" cried Erik.

"It's to slow myself down,"
replied the man. "For I'm the fastest
runner in the world, and if I don't tie up
one of my legs, I'll be at the end of the earth
in a single bounce!"

"Grab hold of this rope, sir," the boy called
down, "and I'll give you a ride in my ship."

So he pulled up the runner, and the ship flew on.

Erik kept a lookout for anyone else on the road below, and at
last he saw a third man. This one had a gun, and he was aiming it
into the distance.

"There's nothing to shoot," yelled the boy, from above. "Only me
and my ship, and we wouldn't want that."

"No, no," the man answered. "I was aiming at a bird on the other
side of the world, for I'm the best shot in the land."

"Are you now?" said Erik, impressed. "Well, come and join us," and
he lowered the rope.

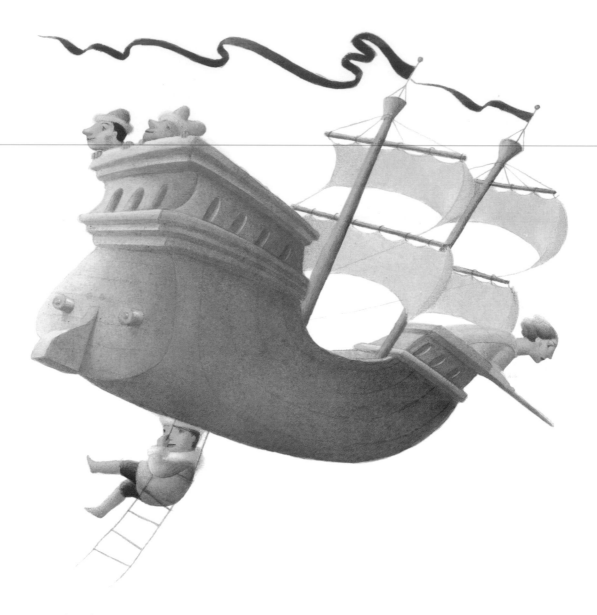

So the finest shot joined the fastest runner and the best listener, and on they flew till they saw another man on the road below, with a basket of bread on his back.

"Where are you off to, sir?" called the boy.

"To fetch some bread for my dinner," answered the man.

"Sure, you've a basketful of it on your back already!" cried Erik, laughing.

"Oh, that's nothing." The man put down the basket and looked inside. "I could finish that lot in one mouthful."

Erik threw him the rope, and the glutton clambered up, into the flying ship.

Then on they flew, till they came to the shore of a great lake, where they saw a fifth man, wandering along the shore, searching.

"What have you lost?" Erik asked him.

"I'm looking for water," the man replied, "for I've a terrible thirst."

"Well, there's a whole lake right there in front of you," said Erik. "Why don't you have some of that?"

"Oh, that'd be no good, boy. I could drink the whole lake down in one gulp, and still be thirsty."

Erik found this hard to believe, but he offered the man a ride in the ship, and up came the mighty drinker.

So the ship flew farther and higher and onward until it was passing over a great forest, and there in a clearing Erik noticed a poor fellow, bent double, with a great bundle of wood above his head.

"Why are you lugging such a bundle, when there's wood all around you?" asked Erik.

"Ah, there's wood and there's wood," said the man. "But the stuff I'm carrying is special."

"How's that?" asked the boy.

"This wood is fighting wood," the man replied. "If you throw it to the ground, it turns into an army of soldiers."

"Well, I've never heard of that!" said Erik. But he threw down the rope and up the man climbed, wood and all.

On they went and on they went, until they saw a seventh man, and this one was carrying a great bale of straw on his back.

"Hello there!" cried Erik. "Where are you going with your straw?"

"I'm going to the next village," answered the man.

"And what's so special about the load on your back?" asked the boy. "For surely there's straw in the village, already."

"Oh, there is, indeed," said the man, "but this straw is magic straw. If you spread it about on a hot summer's day, the air turns cold and everyone shivers."

"What a lot of strange people I'm meeting today," thought young Erik, but he threw down the rope and up came the man, straw and all.

At last the ship, with its very odd crew, arrived at the king's court. The king was in the middle of a great banquet, but when he looked up, he saw it through a window, and sent a courtier out to find out about this strange new bird.

"It's a flying ship, my lord!" whispered the astonished courtier, when he had been out to inspect it. "And it's full of peasants."

The king was delighted to hear that a flying ship had landed in his court, for he had dreamt of seeing one for years. But he was not so pleased with the second bit of news.

"Peasants!" he spluttered into his wine. "I won't have my daughter marrying a humble peasant." For when he had made the offer of his

daughter's hand in marriage to the first person to bring him a flying ship, he had thought that only a rich man, a clever man, a prince from another country, would be able to provide such a wonderful thing.

Then he had an idea. "I know what I'll do," he cried to the assembled company. "I shall set these peasants a series of formidable tasks, and if they cannot carry them out to my satisfaction, I shall have their heads cut off!"

"Good idea, my lord," the courtier smiled. "And what is the first of these tasks?"

"I shall tell them," said the king, stroking his chin, "to fetch me the healing water from the World's End. They must bring it here, to me in my court, before I've even finished my dinner." And, with a dangerous laugh, he began to gobble down the rest of his food.

But the man who could hear everything that was going on in the world had his ear to the ground, and before the king's courtier had even arrived to give Erik the message, he told the boy what was needed.

"How can I do that?" cried Erik. "It would take me a year and a month and a day to fly to the World's End and find the magic water."

"It might," cried the runner, "but I'll have it done in next to no time." He unbound his foot, the one he kept tied up to slow himself down, and was gone in a flash.

He ran and he ran, and in less than a minute he had reached the well at the World's End. He drew up some water into his leather bag, but he was weary from running so fast, so he lay down. "I've time enough for a rest before the king finishes his dinner," he said, closing his eyes. But soon he was dozing, and soon he was snoring and soon he had forgotten why he was even there.

"Where's that mighty runner gone to?" cried Erik, scanning the horizon. "The king will have licked his plate clean by now, and then we'll all have our heads cut off."

So the world's sharpest listener put his ear to the ground once more, and what did he hear but the sound of the runner snoring.

"He's asleep," cried the listener. "Oh, what are we going to do?"

But up stepped the marksman, and he fired a great shot. It flew and it flew till it exploded with a bang right above the runner, there at the end of the world.

"Mercy me!" cried the runner, hearing the great noise and remembering what he was supposed to be doing. "I'd better get moving." So he upped and he ran, and he was back at the ship in next to no time, with the bag of water.

The courtier brought it to the king, who was just about to swallow the last spoonful of his meal. "Oh, fiddlesticks!" he cried, annoyed that his plan had not worked out, and annoyed, too, because he had a pain in his stomach from eating so fast. "I will get my own back on those vulgar peasants. I will set them a task even more impossible."

So he instructed his servant to return to the flying ship and tell the men there that they had to eat, in an instant, twelve of his heaviest oxen and twelve tons of his stodgiest bread.

"Alas and alack," sighed young Erik. "How can we possibly do that? It would take us a year, or the rest of our lives, to eat twelve mighty oxen and twelve tons of bread."

"It certainly won't!" cried the glutton. "Bring them here and I'll gobble them up in under five minutes."

So oxen were roasted, bread was baked and they were delivered to the ship, where he ate every scrap in four and a half minutes flat, just as he had promised. "Not bad for starters," he said, with a belch. "Now, where's the rest?"

"Incredible!" declared the king, when he heard the news. And he locked his only daughter in the tower, for fear he might lose her.

"I shall set them a truly impossible task this time!" he pronounced. "They must drink forty casks, each containing one hundred gallons of wine, and they must do it in three minutes or…"

"Off with their heads?" suggested the courtier.

"Off with their heads!" cried the king, with a wicked laugh.

"Woe is me," groaned the boy, when he heard the news. "It would take us a year and a month and a day, and we wouldn't be able to drink the half of it."

"Not so!" shouted his ever-thirsty comrade. "Bring it here!"

So the wine was brought, and was drunk in two and a half minutes, every last drop of it. "That's better," said the world's biggest drinker, wiping his mouth. "Now where's the rest of it?" But there was not a drop more, for the royal cellars were well and truly empty.

"Astonishing!" declared the king, when he was told, and he ordered that his daughter be tied up in chains, for fear he might lose her to the wild bunch of peasants. Then he had a think, and a thought and a ponder, and he came up with his best plan yet.

"Tell the owner of that flying ship that if he thinks he's going to even meet my daughter, never mind marry her, he'd better have a bath," he ordered. So Erik was summoned, handed a towel and packed off to the royal bathroom.

But the king had a trick up his sleeve. The room was made of iron, and he had ordered that it should be made so hot, and the windows sealed so tight, that the boy would not even be able to breathe.

So when Erik entered the royal bathroom and the door was instantly locked behind him, he discovered that the walls were red hot, and within a few seconds the sweat was streaming off him and he was gasping for breath.

"Never fear, Straw Man is here!" came a voice, and up popped the man with the bale of straw, who had managed to slip into the room before him. He scattered the magical straw all around the floor, and soon the red-hot walls had cooled down and Erik had a delicious bath, neither too hot nor too cold, but perfect.

The king was almost in despair when he heard that the boy had survived this latest scheme to get rid of him, but he thought and he thought, and he came up with one last plan. One last thing a humble peasant could never do. "Tell him to raise me an army, now in an instant!" he demanded.

"And what if he can't?" suggested the courtier, with an evil grin on his face.

"We'll have his head in a bucket!" cried the king.

Well, the sharp-eared comrade had already brought Erik the news, and the boy was desperate. "How can I possibly raise an army? It would take me a year and a month and a..."

"It won't take two minutes," cried the man with the wood on his back. "For surely you haven't forgotten me?"

So when the courtier arrived, with a smirk on his face like the grin of a goblin, Erik told him, "You can wipe that smile off your face, you lackey, for I can raise a better army than your master's got, any day of the week! And you'd better tell him that if he doesn't give me his daughter, as promised, I'll be coming to take her away, whether he likes it or not."

And with that, Erik's friend the woodsman went out into a field, spread his wood around in all directions, gave the mightiest of yells, and up jumped an army — regiment upon regiment of men on horseback! Bugles sounded, drummers drummed, and the king in his castle was terrified.

"Who on earth is this magical boy? I am powerless before him," he moaned, trembling. So he called for his beautiful daughter to be released from her lonely tower, and for a set of royal robes to be given to the boy.

When young Erik came before them, dressed in all his finery, the princess took one look at him and fell head over heels in love. And the king decided he was not so bad after all.

So they were married, the boy and the beauty. All of his family were invited to the celebrations, and orders went out to the ends of the earth for food and wine to be brought. The feast went on for three days and three nights, and even the glutton and the thirsty man had enough to eat and drink.

Rumpelstiltskin

There was once a poor miller, and all he had in the world was his mill by the river and his beautiful daughter. One day he was in town, selling flour, when he got into conversation with the other traders.

"My wife can make the best bread in town," said the egg-man.

"My son can carve a horse's head from a single piece of oak!" cried the carpenter.

"My dog can outrun the fastest hare," boasted the blacksmith.

Not wanting to be beaten, the miller upped and said, "Well, my pretty girl can spin straw into gold."

A hush descended on the crowd, and so he repeated his boast. "Yes, my pretty girl can spin straw into gold!" And then he realized the reason for the hush, for the crowd opened up and there was the king, the mighty king, striding toward him.

"Can she really?" asked the king. "Can your pretty daughter really do as you say?"

"Mmmm… yes, your highness," said the miller, nervously. For you know what it is like — once you are caught in a lie, it is the devil of a job to wriggle out of it.

"Bring her to the palace in the morning, then," the king ordered. "But you'd better be telling the truth."

The poor miller did not dare tell his beloved daughter why she had to go with him, but he did as he was instructed. First thing in the morning he brought her to the palace.

"Aha!" cried the king when he saw her. "She's pretty, I'll grant you that, miller. But we'll soon find out if she can do as you say."

The miller smiled a helpless smile, and the king took the girl by the hand and led her to a chamber, full of straw.

"Get to work," he told her, locking her in. "And if every piece of this straw hasn't been turned into gold by the morning, you're in trouble. Big trouble!"

The poor girl looked around the room, and all she could see was straw, spread about on the floor, and a spinning wheel in the corner, under the window.

"What does he mean? For how can anyone turn straw into gold?" And she crumpled to the floor, her eyes full of tears.

"Stop that crying!" came a squeaky voice. "For the straw will be soaked, and then it'll be no use to man nor beast."

The girl looked up, and there before her stood a tiny little man, with a long, pointy tail. "I have to turn it into gold or the king will have my life," she sobbed.

"Well, what's all the fuss about?" said the little fellow. "I'm sure, if I set my mind to it, I could do it for you in next to no time."

"Could you?" sniffed the girl. "Would you?"

"I could and I would. But what'll you give me if I do?"

"I'll give you this chain." The girl's hand sprang to her neck to unclasp the delicate string of silver that hung there. "It belonged to my dear mother, but I'm sure she wouldn't mind me letting you have it, if it'll save my life."

"She wouldn't, for sure," the little man agreed, and he clasped it in his bony fingers, held it close to his dark little eyes and then stuffed it away, deep in his pocket.

Then down he sat, at the wheel. He fed in the straw and whir, whir, whir, three times round and the bobbin was full. Then he put on a second bobbin, fed in some more straw and whir, whir, whir, till the bobbin was full.

And so it went on, all night until morning. The sound of the whirring sent the miller's daughter into a peaceful sleep, and by the time she awoke the fellow was gone, there was not a speck of straw on the floor and every one of the bobbins was full of gold.

In came the king and when he saw what was there he was thrilled and delighted.

"Hey, hey!" he said, rubbing his hands at the sight of all that shiny gold, gleaming in the early morning sunlight. "That father of yours is more than just a boastful old gasbag, isn't he? He was telling the truth and I'm going to be very rich!"

So he gave the miller's daughter some food and some drink, and then he brought her to another chamber of straw, even bigger than the last, and set her to work again. "You've one single night to turn it all into gold," he warned her. "Or you know what will happen!"

She knew what would happen.

But there was no sign of the little man this time, and the poor girl did not have a clue how he had done what he had done. She sat at the wheel and she fed in the straw but, try as she might, she could not turn it into gold.

The tears were streaming down her face, and it was not from hay fever, when up popped her little friend. "What's the problem, what's the problem?" he squeaked.

"The problem, as you well know," sobbed the girl, "is that if I don't turn every last bit of straw in this here room into gold by sunrise, I'm doomed!"

"Ah, stop your snuffling and move aside, child. I'll see what I can do."

"Would you? Would you, really?"

"I would and I could and I can and I will, if you give me that ring on your finger," and his eyes fixed on the narrow band of silver.

So she gave him her mother's ring, though it made her heart sore to do it, and up he jumped to the wheel. Whir, whir, whir, just as before. All night long, just as before. And by the morning there was no straw and no little man, but the room was full of bobbins of gold and there, before the miller's daughter, was a happy, smiling king.

"Yes!" he cried, throwing his hands in the air. "Soon I'll be the richest man in the whole of the world!"

He gave her food and he gave her drink and then he led her to an even bigger room, full to the brim with straw. "Spin this tonight, and I'll make you my wife," he promised. "Fail in the task, and you're done for!"

When the poor girl was all alone once more, the little fellow upped and popped. "What'll you give me to help you this time?"

"I've given you my chain." She put her hand to her neck. "And I've given you my ring," she added, stroking her empty finger. "I'm afraid I've nothing left, sir."

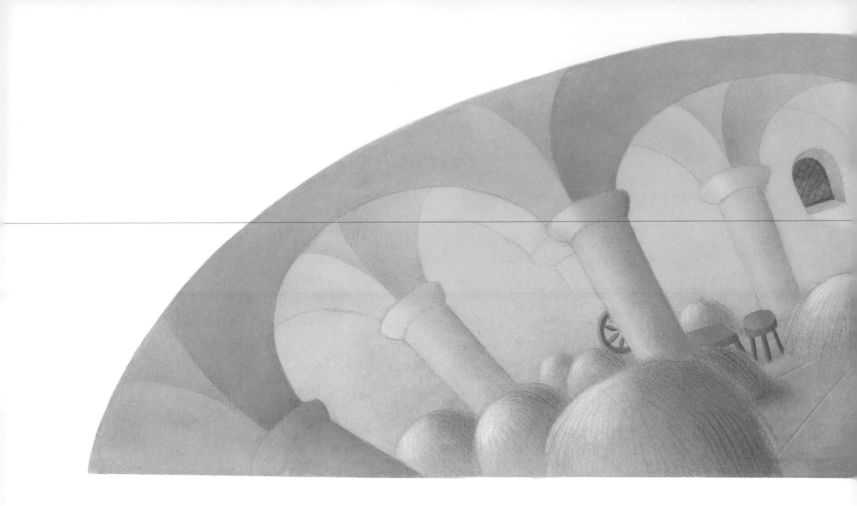

"Oh, it's not what you've got NOW that I want," shrieked the little man. "It's what you might have in the future!"

"What do you mean?"

"Promise to give me your first child!" he hissed. "Your first child when you become queen."

The girl was shocked. But then she thought, and she thought some more. "Who knows if I shall ever even become queen? Who knows if I shall ever even have a baby? Who knows if I shall even be alive tomorrow, unless I agree?" she asked herself.

"Fair enough," she sighed.

"Fair enough, what?" the little man demanded.

"If you turn all the straw in this room into gold by morning," she replied, "you can have my first child if I become queen."

And with a shriek of joy and a spin of his pointy tail, the sly little fellow pushed her off the chair, grabbed a handful of straw and

78

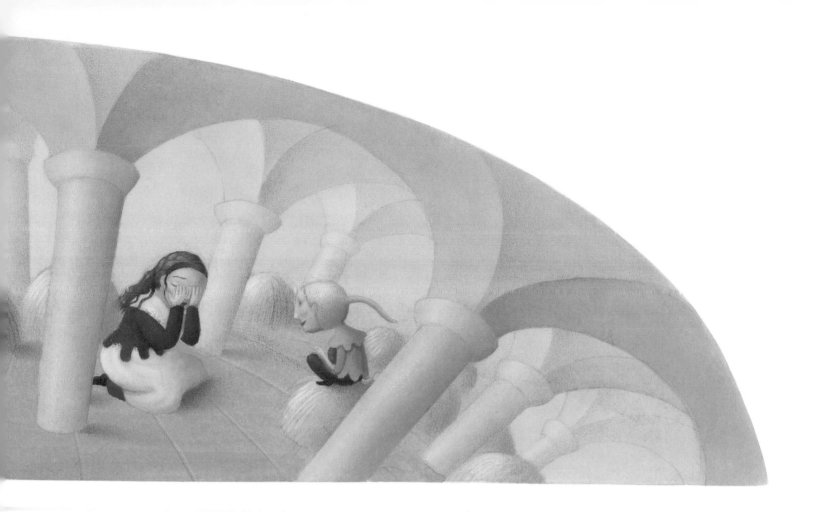

proceeded to spin. Straw into gold, straw into gold, whir, whir, whir.

The girl fell asleep to the sound of the spinning, and in the morning there was no straw and no little man but the room glittered with gold, and there in the open doorway stood the king, thrilled at the sight. "I'm the richest man in the world, and you will be my wife!" he proclaimed.

And from that day on all the greed and the nastiness was gone from him and he was the kindest, most loving husband the miller's daughter could have wished for. They had a wonderful wedding, everything was as it should be, and the new queen was so happy in the days and months that followed that she forgot all about the terrible promise she had made.

But one night she was putting her new, sweet little baby to sleep when suddenly, out of nowhere, the odd little demon appeared. "Aha," he said, his tail twirling with excitement. "A pretty wee boy!"

"Get away from him!" cried the queen, suddenly remembering the bargain she had struck.

"But you promised!" shrieked the tail-twirler, pushing his way past her. "You promised, and now he is mine!"

"Please," the young woman begged, knowing she was no match for the little fellow's magic. "I have riches beyond your every imagining, now that I am queen," for she remembered his fondness for silver. "I will give you them all, if you will only spare my child!"

"But a deal's a deal!" he screamed. "All I ever wanted is a human child all to myself, and now I've got one!" And he reached past her into the cradle with his long, bony fingers and grabbed the baby boy.

"No!" yelled the queen, and she began weeping and wailing so much that even the little man's goblin-heart melted just a tiny bit.

"I'll tell you what," he told her, laying the startled child back in his crib. "I'll give you one chance to keep your pretty baby…" And he grinned a sly little grin.

"What's that?" The queen was desperate. "What must I do?"

"You must guess my name!" he cried, with a shrill little laugh. "But you've only got three days, and if you haven't done it by then, I'm taking what's mine!"

The queen spent the night with her babe in her arms, going over all the names she had ever heard, but not one of them seemed right for the strange little fellow.

"Come to bed, my love," said her husband, but she could not bear to leave the child alone, in case the nasty goblin-creature might change his mind and come back to steal her precious baby.

She sent her faithful companion, her lady-in-waiting, all through the countryside to find any names she might not have heard of before, so that when the little man appeared, at nine o'clock the next day, just

as he said he would, she began: "Is it Caspar, Melchior, Balthazar…?"
And she continued with all the names she had ever heard in her life, in
a great long string.

But the trickster's tail twirled faster with every name she got
wrong, till he was almost flying around the room. "It's not!" he cried,
when she had finished. "It's not any one of them!" And he grinned his
sly little grin, and off he went.

So the queen clutched her baby even tighter and sent her
companion far and wide to find even more names.

"Is it Bandylegs or Gobbletop or Crumpleberger?" she asked when
the little fellow returned the next morning. But he spun his pointy
tail, shook his little head, grinned from ear to ear, and off he went.

Early on the third morning,
the queen's companion came back with a strange
story. "I haven't been able to find a single new name, your highness,"
she told her mistress, "but I was deep in the woods when I heard a
high-pitched singing. I followed the noise until I came to a tiny
cottage. In front of it was a fire, burning, and the funniest little man
singing a song."

"What was he singing?" asked the queen, for she knew at once that
it was her very own little demon. "Tell me what he was singing!"

So her companion sang the song she had heard, in a sly little
high-pitched voice, just like the goblin-man:

"*The secret's mine and I know it's true,*
That tomorrow, my prince, I'll be coming for you.
The queen has lost, and I've won the game,
For Rumpelstiltskin is my name!"

Well, the queen could not believe her luck! She hugged her friend, tears of joy ran down her face, and when the little man appeared, at the stroke of nine, it was her turn to do the teasing. "Are you Jim?" she asked, hiding her smile.

"I'm not," said he, rubbing his hands in excitement.

"Are you Peter, then?"

"No, indeed," he laughed. By now his tail was spinning like a top, and he was over by the cradle, just about to reach in and grab the prize he had been longing for.

"Well, what about… Rumpelstiltskin?" asked the queen.

The little goblin-man gave a terrible scream, fit to wake the dead.

"How did you know?" he shrieked. "A demon must have told you!"

And in a blinding flash he was gone forever. The baby was saved, the queen was delighted and they lived out their lives in peace.

The Sleeping Beauty

O nce upon a time there lived a king and a queen. They lived in a great castle and they were rich beyond compare, yet their lives were filled with sadness, for the one thing they wanted, more than anything else in the world, was to have a child.

One day the queen found herself down by the river. "All I want is a child!" she cried, her eyes filling with tears. "Oh, why can't I have my own child?"

Suddenly up popped a frog, onto a lily pad right in front of her. "Dry your tears, my lady," he croaked, "for you can and you will. Yes, in less than a year, you shall have your very own little daughter." And, with that, he was gone, under the water, away.

The queen could hardly believe the news! In fact, she was so happy that she ran and she skipped all the way back to the castle, waving her arms around and yelling at the top of her voice. "Husband! Husband! We're going to have a baby!"

Well, if the queen was delighted, the king was delirious. He hugged her and kissed her, he laughed and he cried, and sure enough, within a year, a fine baby girl was born.

The king was so
full of pride and so full of joy
that he ordered a great feast. He
invited his sisters and brothers, his
friends and relations and anyone else he
could think of. And, just to make sure that
they did not put a curse on his pretty little
baby, he invited the Twelve Wise Women,
who were in fact fairies.

Unfortunately there were actually thirteen
of them, but the king only had twelve
golden plates, and he did not want the
Wise Women to be arguing amongst
themselves, there at the feast, so he
only invited twelve, which
meant that one of them had
to be left at home.

Well, it was a good
idea, inviting the Twelve
Wise Women, for they
ate and they drank
and they had a whale
of a time, and when
the feasting was over
they offered their gifts
to the little princess,
and very special gifts

they were. For one gave the princess wit, the second gave her beauty, the third gave her grace and the fourth gave her courage, and so they carried on, one after another, offering her everything you could wish for and more.

But maybe it was not such a good idea after all, for just after the eleventh had spoken, in strode the thirteenth, the one who had been left at home, with her face in a deep scowl. "In her fifteenth year," she hissed, pointing her long, bony finger at the pretty little baby, "she will prick herself with a spindle and fall down dead!" And with that, she turned and stomped out of the room.

Everyone shuddered at this terrible curse, but up spoke the twelfth Wise Woman, the one who had not yet given her gift. "Take heart, your majesties," she said. "I cannot undo the curse of my sister, but I will do everything in my power to soften it. It will not be a death, therefore, but a deep sleep of a hundred years into which your beloved princess will fall."

The king, who hoped against hope that he could prevent the curse from taking effect, even in its milder form, sent out orders that every spindle in the kingdom should be destroyed. "Burn your spindles! Burn your spindles, by royal decree!" cried his messengers, all over the land.

And everyone did, for word had spread of the Wise Woman's curse, and no one wanted it to be their spindle that the poor little princess pricked her finger on.

So it came about, in time, that the little girl grew up, beautiful, modest, good natured and wise, so that anyone who met her was bound to love her. But fifteen years is a long time, and though the curse never faded, the memory of it did.

One day, soon after the beautiful princess had reached her fifteenth year, the king and queen and all of their courtiers went out riding, leaving her alone in the castle. She wandered all over, poking around in cupboards and cellars, until at last she came to an old tower she had never noticed before. Up she climbed, up the narrow winding staircase, until she reached a door at the top. There was a rusty key in the lock, and when she turned it the door creaked open, and there in the little room sat an old, old woman with a spindle, spinning flax to make into linen.

"Good day to you, old woman," said the princess. "What is it you're doing?" For, of course, she had never seen such a thing in her life.

"I am spinning, my pretty one," answered the old woman.

"How nice it looks!" cried the princess. "Can I have a go?" And she leaned forward, to take a closer look at how it was done. "What sort of a thing is this, bobbing about?" she asked, touching the spindle. But as soon as she did, the curse of the thirteenth Wise Woman took effect. With a gasp of pain, the princess pricked her finger, and a drop of royal blood dripped to the floor.

"I'm so tired!" she moaned, and she staggered over to the old woman's bed and fell, there and then, into the deepest sleep that anyone has ever slept in the whole history of the world.

And it did not just happen to her, but to every living thing in the castle. The king and queen and all of their courtiers, only just returned from their ride, each fell into the deepest sleep, too. So did the horses in the yard, the dogs in their shed, the pigeons on the roof and the flies upon the wall. Even the fire, blazing in the hearth, died away and slept, the meat stopped sizzling, the cook held off from tugging on the kitchen boy's hair, for she had just been giving him a good talking to for being fresh, and the maid dropped the chicken whose neck she was about to wring and fell asleep, too. Not a leaf stirred, not a bird sang — not a whistle, not a laugh, not a yawn.

And they did not just sleep for a night, and they did not just sleep for a year. No, the curse was for a hundred years — longer than most lifetimes! All around the castle grew a hedge of briars and brambles and thorns, all tangled together so that neither man nor beast could get through. Higher and higher they grew, these thorns, until in time there was nothing to be seen of the castle, not even the flag upon the roof. You would not have any idea there had ever been such a thing, except that the story of the Sleeping Beauty went all around the country, passed down to people's children and their children's children, changing with every telling, until no one was sure any more where exactly it had happened, who it had happened to, or even whether it had really happened at all.

From time to time, though, kings' sons would arrive in the forest, determined to break their way through the wall of thorns, to find out if there was any truth in the tale. Sadly, none of them succeeded. Most of them were in the wrong place altogether, and they wore themselves out hacking and chopping, burning and cutting and never finding so much as a wall. And the ones who were fortunate enough to guess the right spot, were not in fact lucky at all, for the evil thorns grabbed them like claws and held on tightly until each and every one of the poor brave princes died a cruel and horrible death.

After many long years another king's son, from a far distant land, found himself in the forest, purely by chance, and came upon an old man, gathering wood.

"Have you ever heard of the hidden castle?" the old man asked him.

"I have not," said the king's son.

"Have you ever heard of the Sleeping Beauty, who had to stay asleep for a hundred years?"

"I have not," replied the king's son. "And where is this castle and where is this girl?"

"Right there behind you!" The old man pointed. "Right in the middle of that gigantic thorn hedge. Or so my old father once told me. But don't try and go in, young man, or you'll never come out alive!"

Well, the prince was a mighty adventurer, and if he was warned that something was dangerous, then he was certain to try it. So as soon as he heard the old man's words, he drew out his sword and started to hack at the bushes.

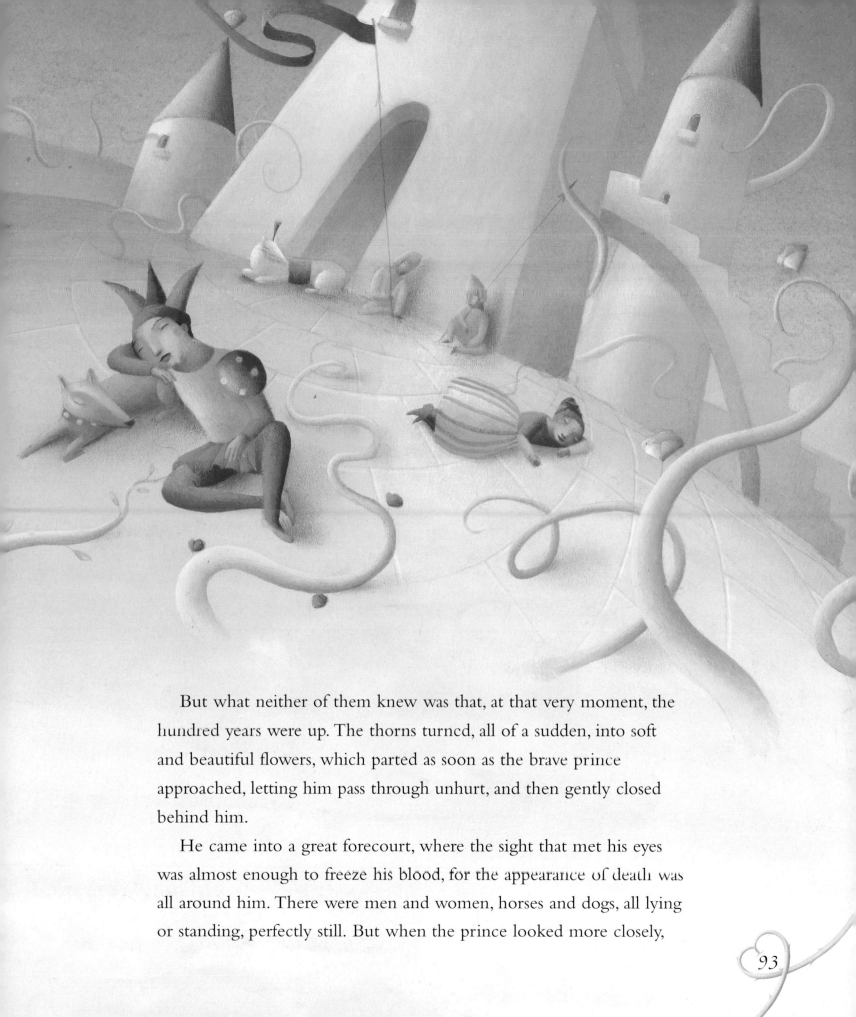

But what neither of them knew was that, at that very moment, the
hundred years were up. The thorns turned, all of a sudden, into soft
and beautiful flowers, which parted as soon as the brave prince
approached, letting him pass through unhurt, and then gently closed
behind him.

He came into a great forecourt, where the sight that met his eyes
was almost enough to freeze his blood, for the appearance of death was
all around him. There were men and women, horses and dogs, all lying
or standing, perfectly still. But when the prince looked more closely,

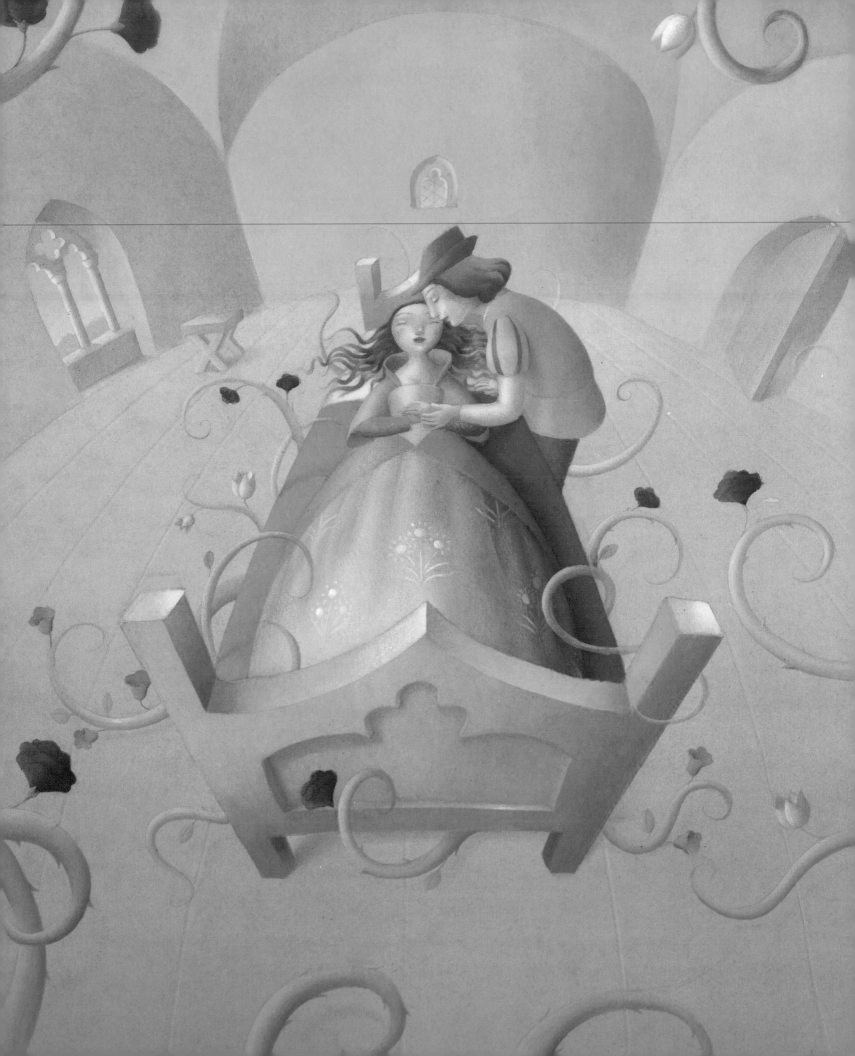

he discovered that every one of them was breathing. Every one of them was asleep!

In the castle yard the horses and hounds still snored, and the pigeons on the roof sat with their heads tucked under their wings. And when the king's son entered the house, the flies were asleep upon the wall, the cook was still holding the kitchen boy's hair and the chicken lay on the floor, where the maid had dropped it.

He went farther in, and in the great hall he saw the whole of the court, asleep, and up by the throne lay the king and the queen.

Even farther in he ventured, while all around him was silence, until at last he came to the mysterious tower. Climbing up the narrow winding staircase, he opened the door into the little room where the princess was sleeping. There she lay, so lovely that he could not turn his eyes away. So captivated was he by her frozen beauty that he stooped down and stole a kiss, and as soon as he did she opened her eyes and smiled up at him.

At that very same moment, the king awoke, the queen awoke and the courtiers opened their eyes wide and stared at one another, amazed. The horses in the courtyard stood up and shook themselves, the hounds jumped up, wagging their tails, the pigeons on the roof flew off, the flies crept over the wall, the fire in the kitchen sparked into flame, the meat began cooking, the chicken gave a mighty squawk and ran around the room and the cook gave the kitchen boy such a yank on his hair that he hollered.

"Will you marry me?" asked the king's son, on bended knee, for he knew, just by looking at the lovely princess, that he could not live without her. And the Sleeping Beauty said that she would.

The celebrations went on for a whole week, and they lived happily, there in the castle in the forest, to the end of their days.

The Jeweled Sea

"You have been a good student, Kwang-Su," said Shun-Che, the great master. "Over these past three years I have taught you all there is to know. It is time for you to go back to your parents and look after them in their old age."

"I shall be sorry to go, master," said Kwang-Su, "for you have been an excellent teacher."

"I am sorry to lose you, also," Shun-Che replied. "But you must leave in the morning. Go by the Indigo Bridge, for there you shall meet your future wife."

"But master!" Kwang-Su was surprised. "I have not been thinking of taking a wife."

"I know," said Shun-Che, with a laugh. "But as soon as you see her, you will be thinking of nothing else."

Kwang-Su rose early the next morning and began the long walk home to Yo-Chan. By the time he reached the Indigo Bridge he was weary, for he had not slept at all well, what with his sadness at leaving his master, his excitement at returning to his parents, and his puzzlement at the words of Shun-Che.

"I will rest here a while," he muttered, and instantly he was asleep. In his dream, a tall and beautiful maiden appeared. She had a red cord tied around one of her feet, and when Kwang-Su looked more closely he saw that the other end of it was tied around one of his own.

"Who are you and what does this mean?" he asked her.

"My name is Ling-Ling," the maiden answered. "When a boy is born, the Fairy of the Moon ties an invisible red cord around his foot, and the other end of the cord around the foot of the girl-baby he is to marry. It can only be seen in sleep."

"So you are the one I am to marry?" whispered Kwang-Su. The girl nodded, and then disappeared.

Kwang-Su, now fully awake, set off down the road, but soon he grew thirsty. Seeing a little house nearby and an old woman sitting in the doorway, he asked her for a drink. The woman called through to her daughter to fetch some water, and who should appear but Ling-Ling.

"It is you!" cried the young man, delighted. "I feared I might never see you again."

"Yes, it is me," replied the girl, laughing.

"How do you know my daughter?" asked the old woman. And Kwang-Su told her how Ling-Ling had appeared to him in a dream that very morning.

The old woman was not surprised, for it was she who had given Ling-Ling the power to step in and out of people's dreams. But she was not pleased either, for she could see straight away that Kwang-Su and Ling-Ling had fallen in love.

"I cannot let you marry her," she insisted, "for a rich mandarin is anxious to make her his wife."

"But I've told you before, mother!" cried Ling-Ling. "I do not want to marry that wrinkled old man, for he has a face like a monkey! And besides, the Fairy of the Moon did not tie my foot to his."

"That is true," said her mother, sighing, and she knew that she had a problem. For the sake of the family, it was important that Ling-Ling married the richest man she could. But if the Fairy of the Moon really had tied Kwang-Su and Ling-Ling's feet together, then it was most dangerous to interfere.

She called Kwang-Su into the house. Surprised by the fragrant smell that greeted him, he looked around the room. Herbs were strewn all over the floor, and on a stool in the middle lay a broken pestle and mortar.

"With this pestle and mortar," the old woman told him, "I pound magic potions from the genies. But, now that they are broken, I cannot do it any more."

"I could buy you new ones in the city," suggested Kwang-Su.

98

"Thank you," replied the woman, "but that would not help, for to do justice to their magic they have to be made of jade, and the only way to replace them is to go to the home of the genies, high on a mountain above the Jeweled Sea. If you will do that, Kwang-Su, and bring me back a jade pestle and mortar, I shall be happy to let you marry my daughter."

Kwang-Su had no idea where the genies lived, but Ling Ling took him out into the garden and pointed to a distant range of snowcapped mountains.

"The highest is Mount Fumi," she told him. "The genies sit on top, looking down on the Jeweled Sea. It is a fabulous place, of uncountable riches, but no human has ever been there and returned to tell the tale."

"I will go," offered the boy. "Just tell me how to get there."

"First you must cross the Blue River," said the girl, "then the White River, the Red River and finally the Black River."

"That will be easy, then, for I am an excellent swimmer."

"I'm afraid it won't," she warned him. "Each river is full of monstrous creatures, who would eat you as soon as you entered the water. That is why my mother has given you this task. She thinks you will never come back alive, and that it will then be safe for me to marry the rich mandarin."

"So what can I do?" asked the boy. "How can I fetch the jade pestle and mortar?"

"Take my magic box." Ling-Ling handed him a tiny wooden container. "In it are six red seeds. Throw one in each river as you pass, and it will shrink to a tiny stream, over which you can easily jump."

Kwang-Su was determined to marry Ling-Ling, despite the risk, so he took the box, kissed her good-bye, and away he went. On his way he passed through the town of Yo-Chan, where his parents lived, and he went and told them all that had happened since he had left home.

"I don't think the genies will be very happy to see you turning their mighty rivers into streams," his mother warned him, for she was a wise woman, as mothers usually are. "If you want them to let you have a jade pestle and mortar, I think you'd better take these."

And she handed him a second tiny box, and this one contained six

white seeds. "Throw one into each stream after you've crossed back over on your way home, and it will become a river again."

In the morning Kwang-Su kissed his father and mother and went on his way. He rested in the midday heat, carried on when it grew cool, and at the end of seven days he came to the Blue River. It was a quarter of a mile wide, as blue as the midsummer sky, and the most terrifying fish were popping out of the water in every direction. The head of every fish was twice the size of a football, and each one had the sharpest teeth Kwang-Su had ever seen.

But he was not frightened, for he trusted Ling-Ling and the power of her little red seeds. Opening the box, he pulled one out and tossed it into the waters as they lapped against the shore. Right away, the wide blue river became a gentle stream, the man-eating creatures were no bigger than tadpoles, and Kwang-Su hopped safely across the water.

Not long after, he came to the White River, and even though he had had such success before, this one stopped him in his tracks. It was half a mile wide, the water foamed and bubbled as it rushed past, and everywhere, under the surface and over, were the most immense and terrifying sea serpents.

But Kwang-Su knew what to do. He pulled out the second red seed and threw it into the water. To his great delight, the raging river again shrank to a trickle and the mighty creatures became nothing more than the tiniest of eels.

Hopping across, the young man carried on, whistling as he went, until he reached the Red River. This one took his breath away, for it was three-quarters of a mile wide, it looked like a sea of blood, and a row of angry alligators, jaws open wide, stretched across it like a bridge.

"Now for my third little seed!" he cried, opening his box.

Snap went the jaws of the nearest alligator as the seed flew through the air, but the dreadful creature missed it and soon found itself no bigger than a lizard, wallowing at the bottom of a gentle brook.

"Who dares to shrink our mighty rivers?" came a terrible roar, and Kwang-Su looked up to see a genie, towering high above him.

"It's all right, sir," the boy stammered, pulling out the box of little white seeds his mother had given him. "As soon as I've done what I've come to do, I'll throw one of these into each of your mighty rivers, and they'll be as big and strong as ever they were."

"They'd better be, boy," warned the genie, scowling. "Or it'll be the end of you. Now what is it that brings you here?"

"I've come to find a jade pestle and mortar for my future mother-in-law to pound her magic potions in."

"You've another river to cross, then," the genie laughed. "And I don't see how a tiny seed will help you over it for it's the Black River,

102

a mile wide, and it's full of the mightiest fish with spikes on their backs like porcupines."

"So how did you get across, if it's so difficult?" asked the boy.

"Oh, it's no bother to me," chuckled the genie. "I can fly."

"Well, I can jump," said Kwang-Su, with a smile, and off he went.

The genie — who was only a young genie, as it turned out — went after him, and they set off together for the Black River. But when they got there Kwang-Su's heart sank, for what did he see but a great expanse of roaring water, as black as ink, stretching out in front of him for as far as the eye could see, and the sharpest of spikes sticking up and out, all over.

He did not want the genie to know that he was afraid, so, with a great flourish, he pulled out the box of seeds, pitched the fourth one into the seething water and watched it disappear beneath a coal-black wave. In an instant the river dried up, leaving only a shallow pool at Kwang-Su's feet, with the fish no bigger than sea urchins.

The genie was much impressed by the boy's magic, so he offered to take him to the summit of Mount Fumi. It was a long, hard climb, but Kwang-Su was determined to get there. Eventually he reached the top of the glorious mountain, where he found eight old and mighty genies, each on his own snow-clad peak, looking down on the fabulous Jeweled Sea, which stretched out below them on the other side.

Kwang-Su stared at the beautiful sheet of water, flashing in the sun with every color of the rainbow. He forgot all about the pestle and mortar as he watched the waves rippling on the shore, washing up diamonds and rubies, sapphires and pearls. Every single pebble was a precious stone, and Kwang-Su wanted nothing more than to go down to the shores of the beautiful lake and fill his pockets with them.

Meanwhile the young genie who had been his guide explained to the others why the boy had come, and told them about the wonderful red and white seeds that he carried with him. "We must allow him the pestle and mortar," he told them, "or he won't give us our rivers back."

The eight venerable genies knew that their younger friend was right, for it was the might of the giant rivers that prevented any human from ever reaching the Jeweled Sea. They were angry, though, for they did not like the idea of a puny human with a few tiny seeds having greater power than them.

"Let him have them, then," cried one, his voice like the rumble of thunder among the hills. "If he can carry them!"

And all eight of the mighty genies laughed and laughed until the snow-clad peaks shook beneath them. For it turned out that the mortar made of jade was bigger than a man, and the pestle was so heavy that no human could ever hope to lift it.

When Kwang-Su had finished gazing at the Jeweled Sea, he walked around the pestle and mortar and wondered how on earth he could carry them back down the mountain and across the plains to Yun-Nan. He sat down beside them, to think the matter over, while the eight mighty genies chuckled away.

"Take them if you can," said one, teasing him. "And why not fill the mortar with precious stones while you're at it? For any man who can carry it empty can carry it full."

Kwang-Su sat there, thinking. He had not studied for three years with the wisest master in the land for nothing, and besides, he was determined to marry Ling-Ling.

His ears had been closed to the genies while he thought, for he knew they were only mocking him, but slowly, slowly, their words filtered through to his brain. Fill the mortar with precious stones, one had said. And suddenly Kwang-Su had an idea.

"Would you do me a favor?" he asked the younger genie. "Would you make a heap of stones at the side of my mortar?"

"Why?" asked his friend.

"I want to look inside it, and I'm not tall enough to see over the rim."

"Fair enough," replied the genie, and he began to build some steps for the young man to climb. Meanwhile Kwang-Su ran down to the water and started stuffing his pockets with diamonds and rubies, emeralds and pearls. When he had gathered up as many as he could carry, he ran back up the mountain, climbed the steps the young genie had made for him and emptied the precious stones into the mortar.

Again and again he did this until it was quite full, and held enough gems to make him the richest man in China, richer even than the wealthiest mandarin.

When he had filled the mortar so full that he could not fit one more stone in, he stood back and admired his haul.

"So what are you going to do with it now, boy?" asked one of the mighty genies, watching him. "Take it on your head and carry it home?"

"No," replied the boy, with a smile. "I shall carry it under one arm." And with that, he took out his little box, dropped one of the remaining red seeds on top of the precious stones, and in a moment the pestle and mortar shrank to normal size. Then Kwang-Su picked up the pestle, slipped it into his pocket, and lifted the mortar as carefully as he could, so as not to spill the jewels.

"Good-bye," he said, bowing to the astonished genies, "and thank you for allowing me to take home so many of your riches." And off he trotted, scarcely believing his luck.

Behind him he heard a mighty roar, as if a hundred and eighty lions were waiting to be fed. The genies were furious at being tricked, but they knew better than to stop the boy, for only he had the power to turn the four tiny streams back into mighty rivers.

Kwang-Su did exactly as he had promised. He jumped across the first brook, threw one of the white seeds his mother had given him into the water, and instantly it turned back into an inky black waste, a mile wide,

full of enormous spiky fish. The roars of the genies ceased when they saw
the Black River rolling once more between them and the outside world.

At the Red River, the White River and the Blue River, Kwang-Su
did just the same, and from that day to this no one else has ever been
to the home of the genies, because not a single person could cross even
one of those raging rivers.

For seven more days he journeyed on, and he came at last to his
parents' home in Yo-Chan. Well, weren't they delighted to see their
only son, safe and well! And when he gave his mother a precious stone
for every seed she had given him — a diamond, a ruby, an emerald, a
pearl, a sapphire and a pink topaz, each as large as a robin's egg — they
were over the moon.

He went on, then, all the way to Yun-Nan, to find and marry his
beloved Ling-Ling.

"Go away, boy!" hissed the girl's mother, when she opened the door and saw who it was. "You're too late!"

"What do you mean, I'm too late?" cried Kwang-Su, in a fury. "I have crossed the mightiest rivers, scaled the highest mountains, faced the angriest genies, and fetched you back the jade pestle and mortar you asked for. And not only that," he said, pulling out piles of precious stones from his pockets, "I have brought you these! Look, I am now richer than the richest mandarin! How dare you say I am not fit to marry your daughter?"

"Oh dear," said the woman, all confused. "I never thought you would return. All my friends are gathered here, in the garden, to honor Ling-Ling's marriage to the rich mandarin."

"And are they married yet?"

"No," replied the old woman, "the ceremony is just beginning."

Kwang-Su pushed past her, raced out into the garden and shouted "STOP!" at the very top of his voice.

Everyone turned to look, and Ling-Ling almost fainted when she saw who it was. "My mother told me you were dead!" she cried, falling into his arms. And Kwang-Su almost fainted when he saw her too, for she was so beautiful in her pink silk wedding dress, embroidered in silver, and at the very sight of her, he fell in love all over again.

"You are too late!" Ling-Ling's mother hissed, rushing over to them. "The mandarin would be furious with me, and all my guests would think I am a fool. Just go away, Kwang-Su! Leave quietly, and I will buy the jade pestle and mortar from you with some of the money the rich mandarin has given me."

"No!" cried Kwang-Su, and he dropped one of the little white seeds into the mortar, which grew in size instantly, until it filled the plot of grass beneath the peach tree and was full to overflowing with glittering jewels.

Then he climbed up into the tree and threw down, all among the wedding guests, rubies and diamonds and all kinds of precious stones. Most just stood and stared, but a few scrambled about on the ground, grabbing as many as they could, and the busiest of all was the monkey-faced mandarin.

"How greedy he is," said the others, watching. "You wouldn't think, to look at him, that he was already one of the richest men in China, and that even his teacups are set with diamonds."

Then Kwang-Su offered the greedy mandarin his three largest rubies, each the size of a hen's egg, if he would go away and think no more about marrying Ling-Ling ever again. And the mandarin, who cared much more for riches than for love, agreed.

So Kwang-Su and Ling-Ling were married soon after, in the city of Yo-Chan, where his mother and father lived. Most of the riches Kwang-Su had brought back from the Jeweled Sea were given to the poor of the city, and the boy and girl were as happy as two young people deserve to be when they love each other dearly.

The Celestial Sisters

Waupee was a great hunter and, although he was still young, he could run faster and shoot straighter than anyone else in his tribe. He had eyes that could see in the darkest forest, and he could follow any trail, no matter how cold.

The forest where Waupee lived was full of birds and animals, and every morning he would go out with his knife and his bow, and every evening he would return with food enough to share.

One strange day, when there was no prey to be seen, he came to the edge of the woods and found himself on the prairie. It was a wide plain, covered with long blue grass and many-colored flowers. This was the first time Waupee had ever set foot outside the great forest so he traveled on, enjoying the open country and the fragrant breeze, until he came to a sudden halt. For there in front of him was a circle of flattened grass, with another ring around it as though made by the lightest of feet.

"How can this be?" he muttered, for there was no sign of any path leading to the circle, not a trace of a footstep, not a broken twig, not even a crushed leaf. "I shall hide in the long grass," he said, "and wait to see what creature it is that could have made these marks."

He hid in total silence, not moving an inch, until at last he heard faint sounds of music in the air. Looking up, he saw a strange object, floating in the sky like a summer cloud. At first it seemed so small that Waupee thought it might be blown away by the slightest breeze, but as he watched it approach it grew bigger and bigger, and the music came clearer and more sweetly to his ear.

As it neared the earth, he could see that it was a great floating basket and that inside were twelve sisters, each of the most enchanting beauty. As soon as the basket settled on the ground, the sisters leaped out and began to dance around the magic circle, throwing from one to another a shining ball, from which came the most exquisite melodies.

Waupee gazed with delight at the scene before him. Each sister seemed more attractive than the one before, but the most beautiful of all was the youngest, and he fell in love with her right away.

He rushed forward to tell her, but the twelve sisters, as soon as they saw him, cried out in fear. They ran to the basket, leaped in and were drawn up at once into the sky.

Waupee watched them leave, sadness filling his heart. "They are gone forever," he said, and he returned to his lodge, where he spent the night staring at the sky. But the very sight of it brought further sadness, for it had stolen the only girl he had ever loved.

The next day he set off through the woods, in the hope of finding the sisters once more. He followed the same trail as before, and even though there were birds and animals all around this time, he did not stop. Now that he had seen the woman of his dreams, the only thing on his mind was to find her again and to tell her he loved her.

So he went on, right through the great forest until he reached the open space of the prairie. Hardly noticing the blue of the grass and the fragrance of the flowers, on he went, until he arrived at the very same spot he had been the day before, at the very same time. He hid in the long grass near the rings, but fearing that the mysterious sisters would not appear if they sensed that he was there, he took the form of an opossum, with a long, pointy snout.

He had not waited long when he saw the basket descend, and heard the same sweet music. But the instant the sisters caught sight of him, even as an opossum, they sprang into their basket and rose out of sight.

Then Waupee, casting off his animal form, walked sorrowfully back to his lodge, and once again the night was long, so long, for he was filled with thoughts of the beautiful girl he had lost. The next day he returned to the enchanted spot, hoping beyond hope that the maiden might reappear. Searching the grass, he spotted a family of mice and he decided there and then to become a mouse himself, for that way he would be less likely to alarm the celestial sisters.

Waupee nibbled and squeaked and ran about with the others, but he remembered to keep his sharp eyes watching and his pointy ears listening for any changes in the sky. Soon enough, down came the sisters and they began their musical dance once more.

"Look!" cried the youngest, bending the grass to show the others. "A family of mice!" But her sisters thought she was silly to be bothered with such things. They laughed and chased the mice away, leaving only Waupee standing there before them. For, in a second, he had returned to his human form and taken the girl he loved in his arms.

"Run!" cried the eldest sister, and she and her sisters rushed to the basket, into the air and away. But it was too late for the youngest. She was held firm and could not escape.

"I will not harm you," Waupee said, wiping away her tears. "Stay with me and be my bride." And he told her of his home and of the charms of life on earth.

With her sisters gone, the youngest knew there was now no way for her to return to the stars, and somehow she found herself strangely drawn to this man before her. So Waupee led her to his lodge and, from that moment on, he was the happiest of men.

Winter and summer passed, and as spring approached their contentment was increased by the birth of a son. He had his mother's beauty and his father's courage and strength.

Waupee gave thanks to the mighty spirits for all that had happened, but his wife was a daughter of the stars, and by the time she had seen everything there was to see and had done everything there was to do, she began to lose interest in being on earth. More and more she missed her father, her sisters and all the joys of her previous life. Although she hid these feelings from her husband, for he was kind to her and she did not wish to hurt him, the pain of being away from

her homeland grew greater

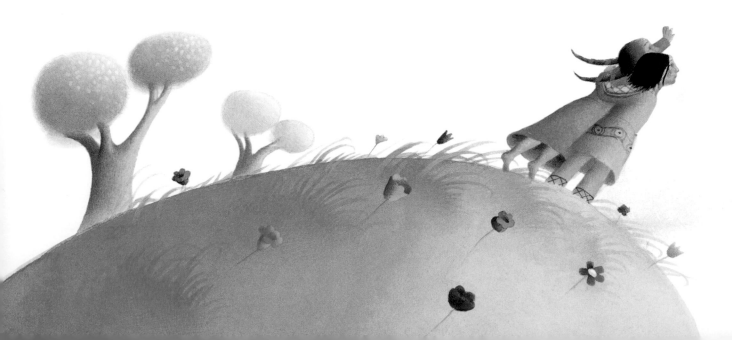

by the hour. So one day, while Waupee was out hunting, she began to construct a wicker basket, which she kept well hidden from her husband. In the meantime, she began to collect things from earth that she thought might please her father, as well as all her favorite earthly foods.

Then, on a day when everything was ready and she believed that her husband was far from home, she took her son with her to the charmed ring. As she helped him into the basket, she began to sing her magical song, and they rose into the air.

The song was sad, for it was a song of leaving, and the wind carried it across the prairie and into the forest, where Waupee heard it. Recognizing the voice of his beloved wife, he raced at lightning speed through the forest and arrived at the magical ring just as the basket rose into the sky. "Do not leave me!" he cried, frantically trying to grab hold of the trailing ropes. But it was too late.

"How can I live without you, my love?" he wailed, hoping his wife might take pity on him and somehow return to the ground. But there was no reply. The basket continued to climb, up and up, until it was only a tiny speck, and then it disappeared from view.

When the young woman arrived at her home in the stars, her father and sisters were delighted to see her again and thrilled to meet her little son. Over the course of the days and weeks, months and years that followed, she nearly forgot about her earthly husband, the home they had made together and the life she had left behind.

Her son, though, as he grew up, became more and more like Waupee. He enjoyed his new life, up in the heavens, but every day he became more restless. "When can we visit my father?" he would ask. "When can I go and see the land where I was born?"

His mother was reluctant to take him, for even though some part of her missed Waupee and loved him still, she knew that she could not live on earth and feared that if her son ever set foot there, he might refuse to return.

The child's grandfather took pity on him, however. "A boy should know his father," he said one day. "Take him down to meet him, and ask your mighty hunter if he would like to come up here and visit us."

"I don't think he would, father," replied the woman. "For he loves his lodge and his forest, and most of all he loves his hunting."

"Tell Waupee that his fame as a hunter has spread even to the stars," pronounced the old man. "Ask him to bring with him some part of each bird or animal he hunts, for I should like to see evidence of his many talents."

His daughter, knowing that her earthly husband was a proud man,

thought that this might tempt him to visit her home in the stars, so she agreed. She took her boy, climbed into the basket once more, and off they went, back down to earth.

Waupee, who came every day to the enchanted spot where he had first met the woman he still loved, was hunting near the edge of the forest. Hearing her joyful song, he rushed to the ring, to be there as she descended. His heart beat with happiness as he saw that it was indeed his beloved wife, and soon she was in his arms once more.

"And is this my son?" he cried, looking at the boy. "What a fine young man he has become!"

His wife told him what her father had said, and Waupee thought long and hard about whether he would like to visit the land beyond the sky. In time he decided that he would, and so they agreed to stay with him while he began to hunt in earnest, determined to assemble a fine collection to present to his father-in-law when he met him.

He spent whole nights, as well as days, searching for every example of bird and animal that the forest and prairie had to offer. Some of the catch he prepared for his newfound family to eat, but he always kept a foot, a wing or a tail of each creature to show to the old man.

When all was ready, Waupee visited once more each of his favorite spots, for there was no telling how long he would be away. "This is where I used to watch the rising sun," he told his son, at the top of the highest hill. "And this is where my grandfather taught me how to catch fish," he said, standing by the stream where he had played as a boy.

He said a tearful good-bye to the old lodge, and they made their way to the magic circle. Then, taking his wife and son by the hand, Waupee climbed into the basket and untied the ropes. It was the oddest feeling for him, to be rising from the ground and watch his land slipping away below him. To see the blue grasses of the prairie, the many-colored flowers and then the forest, his beloved forest, growing smaller by the second. How strange to be looking down on it from above. How strange to see all those magnificent trees melting into a great blur of green; to see the trails he used to take, the rivers he used to cross, and to be rising, ever rising, higher than the birds, higher even than the mighty eagle.

Breathless with the beauty of it all, Waupee was silent as they soared upward, ever upward, until he was higher even than the great mountain; until he could see that his forest was only one of many forests; until he could see a great expanse of water, stretching in every direction; until they disappeared into a band of cloud and could see no more. And then, soon after, they were breaking through the cloud into a land stranger than any he had ever dreamed of, a land of blueness, of brightness, of nothing but sun.

There was great joy when they arrived in
the land of the stars. The chief invited
his people to a feast, and when they
had all gathered together, he spoke.
"Listen closely, my friends," he
announced. "In honor of my
guest, Waupee, I am giving you
a choice. You may continue to
live here, in the heavens, as you
have always done, or you may
select one of the precious gifts
you see before you, and
henceforward live on earth." And
there, laid out in front of them, was the
evidence of Waupee's skill as a hunter —
the wings and claws of birds, the tails and feet
of mighty animals.

   "But I must warn you," said the old man to his
people, while they rushed forward to examine the collection,
"Whatever animal or bird you choose, that is what you will become!"

The people of the stars had never seen such wonderful things before, and they did not heed their leader's warnings. Every one of them chose from Waupee's gifts, and those who selected tails or feet were changed into animals and ran off down to earth, while others became birds and flew into the sky.

Waupee knew what he wanted to be. He picked up three hawk's feathers, offering one each to his wife and son, for he had long dreamed of flying like a bird above his beloved forest, and his favorite had always been the hawk, the mighty hunter.

He greatly feared that they might not agree to join him, but each of them took hold of the feather he offered and instantly they became three hawks, with the very sharpest of talons and the very whitest of wings.

Together they descended with each of the other birds, almost to earth. And there they are still to be found, with the brightness of the starry plains in their eyes and the freedom of the heavenly breezes in their wings.

The Magic Ball

Many long years ago there was a cold-eyed witch, living high in the Andean Mountains. All through the summer she slept in a cave, but every year, as soon as the first snows of winter fell, she awoke.

"Aha!" she would cry, grinning at the frozen land all around her, for there was nothing she loved more than the winter moon, the trees hung with snow, the land all white and the waters icebound and black. "It's hunting time again! Time to find me a juicy little human!" And she would pull from her deep, deep pocket a bright and shiny ball of many colors and she would cackle. Oh, how she would cackle!

Natalia and Luis were sister and brother, and on the first day of winter they were out playing, not far from their home in the foothills of the great mountains. Natalia saw a brightly colored ball and ran to pick it up but, much to her surprise, it began to roll. It went a little way and then it stopped, so she ran after it, laughing, but just before she got there it began to roll again.

"Where are you going?" Luis asked her. He was a year older and always kept an eye on his younger sister.

"I'm trying to catch the pretty ball," she told him, pointing at it. "But every time I reach it, it runs away."

"Don't be silly," said Luis. "I'll fetch it for you." But the same thing happened to him. He ran and he ran, and little Natalia chased after him, but each time he tried to pick up the ball it started to roll again. And there was something else very strange, for it did not just roll downhill, like balls usually do, but uphill as well.

All afternoon they chased it, and they would soon have grown tired of the game, but the ball was a clever ball and every so often it stopped by a bush full of the tastiest berries, or by a crystal-clear spring, so the children, while they rested, had something good to eat and drink. But then, just as they were about to pick up the ball and take it home, off it rolled again.

At last, still following it, Natalia and Luis came to a place in the valley where the River Chico runs between great hills.

The land was covered with mighty chunks of broken rock, and snowflakes appeared in the dark, gloomy air.

"Where are we?" asked Luis, realizing that they were lost. But the ball still rolled, and the children felt strangely drawn to follow it, even though it led them higher and higher up the cold mountain.

Eventually they arrived at a large black rock, where the ball came to rest. Natalia went to pick it up, as she had tried to do so many times before, and this time, much to her surprise, it did not roll away. "Caught you!" she cried, clasping it in her hands, but no sooner had she stared into its swirling colors than the ball vanished, like the popping of a bubble.

The poor girl burst into tears, for she was worn out with all the chasing, and she had so wished to keep the lovely ball that she had spent all afternoon trying to catch. All she wanted was to bring it home to show her father and her mother, and then to give it to her baby brother to play with.

"Never mind," said Luis, trying to console her. "Let's go back down the mountain. It's time to go home." Taking her by the hand, he realized that she was cold, so cold. So he led her around to the other side of the rock, wanting to give her a chance to warm up a little out of the chilly wind before they set off on the long journey home. Natalia curled up in the shelter of the rock and was soon fast asleep.

Luis kept watch, as there was something eerie about the place, but with the pine trees nodding all around him, and the branches soughing in the wind, he soon fell asleep, too.

Little Natalia, sheltered from the bitter wind, was dreaming of home. The warm firelight danced on the walls, lighting up her father's face as he sat mending a saddle. Her mother, she thought, was brushing her hair and singing to her, but then, for some reason, she grew rough and careless. She pulled her daughter's hair, causing Natalia to give a sharp cry of pain and wake up.

In a flash, she knew where she was, chilled to the bone from the piercing wind sweeping down from the mountaintop. She tried to get up, but she could not, for something dreadful had happened. While she and her brother were sleeping, the wicked witch of the Andes, whose magic ball had led the children to her lair, had crept up on them. Stroking and brushing Natalia's hair, she had used her evil powers to bind it into the rock so tightly that the poor little girl could not even turn her head.

"Help me! Help me, Luis!" she cried, stretching out her arms to her brother. "I cannot move!"

But Luis was unable to reach her, for the witch had made an invisible wall around Natalia and the rock, and even though he could see his sister, crying out in pain, he was unable to pass through. "I can't, Natalia! There must be magic in this place, for I cannot get to you. There's some sort of wall blocking me."

"Can't you climb over it?" she pleaded.

"I've reached as high as I can, but it seems to go on forever."

"Come around to the other side, Luis. I'm cold and frightened, here by myself." Natalia wept quietly, her tears turning to ice as they fell.

Suddenly a great white owl flew overhead, singing the strangest song as it went:

"*Things of the dark and things without name*

Save us from light and the torch's red flame."

"Did you hear the owl, Luis?" cried Natalia. "Did you hear what it was singing?"

"I did," said her brother. "But what does it mean?"

"Maybe it's telling us that the magic in this horrible place is afraid of fire. Maybe if you go off and find some, we can escape," said Natalia.

"But I can't leave you here on your own!" cried the boy.

Just then a mighty condor swooped low over the rock, calling:

"Fleet of foot and quick of breath!

Fire will conquer frosted death."

"The condor says the same thing," cried Natalia. "Go now, brother! Go quickly, and find fire before it's too late!"

So Luis waved her a sad farewell and set off down the mountain. He kept an eye on the mighty bird and, deciding that it must be guiding him, he followed it down to the river, until he came to the place where the waters meet.

There he saw a house, a poor little dwelling made of earth and stones. No one was around, but as the condor flew off, high into the sky, until it was nothing but a speck in the air, Luis knew that it was telling him to wait by the house.

Pushing open the door, he could see by the ashes in the fireplace that the owner would soon return, for the embers were well covered to keep the fire alive. So although he was tired and desperately worried for his poor sister, all alone on the mountain, Luis went to fetch fresh water from the spring, gathered wood and piled it neatly by the fire, and then he blew on the embers, adding sticks until bright flames flickered.

Soon the owner of the house came back, and seeing what the boy had done, he gave him some bread and yerba tea. They were silent while they ate, and then the man said, "The white witch of the Andes is a wicked woman, and there is only one way to defeat her. Can you tell me what it is, boy?"

Luis knew nothing about the witch, but he thought he might have the answer.

"Fire will conquer frosted death, sir," he said. "Or that's what the condor told me, anyway."

The old man nodded. "And here he comes, our friend the condor, who sees far and knows much." He pointed to the doorway, where the mighty bird was hovering and calling out:

"*Now, with cold, grows faint her breath,*

But fire will conquer frosted death."

"He's talking about my sister!" cried the boy. "She's dying!"

And with that, the man pulled a lighted branch from the fire and handed it to Luis. "Take this and run, boy! Run and save her!"

So off Luis raced with the blazing stick, through marsh and swamp and any obstacle in his way. Coming to a fast-flowing stream, he ran straight through it, not wanting to lose time by looking for a shallow place to cross.

Wading through the waist-high water, he tried to hold the stick high above his head, but the water splashed the branch and the flame went out.

"Oh, why am I so stupid?" he cried, and he turned and ran all the way back to the little house. "Help me, sir!" he yelled, bursting in through the door. "My fire went out and if I don't reach her soon, my poor sister will be frozen to death!"

So the old man pulled another stick from the fire, handed it to him, and Luis rushed off, vowing to find a safe place to cross the stream this time.

As he ran, the condor swooped low, repeating the words of before:

"Now, with cold, grows faint her breath,

But fire will conquer frosted death."

Luis ran like the wind, up the river, around a lake and high into the frozen mountains. But he tripped on a rock, hidden beneath the snow, and the flaming torch hissed as it hit the floor and went out.

The boy was furious with himself for being so careless, yet there was nothing for it but to go all the way back down to the little house and beg for a third chance to save his sister.

As the old man handed him another burning stick, the condor once more appeared in the doorway, crying:

"Fainter now, the maiden's breath.

Night must bring her frosted death."

The condor rose once more into the sky, and Luis ran like there was no tomorrow, up the river, around the lake and high into the mountains. He held the stick so tightly that it scorched his fingers, but he would not relax his grip for fear of dropping it again.

A flamingo, seeing him, came over and ran alongside. Luis put his free hand on its back and, with the help of the long-legged bird, he was able to run at its speed. Suddenly the flamingo rose into the air, taking Luis with it. The blazing fire from his torch burned its neck and breast until it glowed bright red, but it was the bravest of birds and it carried on regardless.

Straight up the valley it flew, to poor little Natalia. Seeing the frozen girl cowering under the rock, her hair bound like glue to the stone, Luis dropped the blazing stick into a heap of dried moss on the far side. Up leapt the dancing flames and with a tremendous crack the rock exploded into a thousand pieces.

There was a horrible shrieking sound and Luis feared for his dear sister. But then he realized that such a foul noise could not have come from Natalia, not even if she were dying. No, it was the sound of the white witch of the Andes, shrieking in horror as her power was destroyed. Her cry filled the air and then slowly trailed off, as she was banished for ever from those lands.

As for Natalia, there was not a scratch on her. She stood up and with her cold, cold hand stroked the flamingo's burnt feathers. The bird was healed, but as a sign of its bravery it has carried a crimson breast ever since.

Natalia and Luis found their way home and lived many happy years in the green valley. The birds of the mountains were their friends, but the magic ball and the wicked witch were never seen again.

Snow-white and Rose-red

A poor widow once lived in a little cottage, and in her garden grew two rose trees, one white and one red. She had two daughters who were just like the trees, for one had skin as white as snow, and the other always had rosy-red cheeks.

Rose-red loved to run all around the fields and meadows, picking flowers and chasing butterflies, but Snow-white preferred to stay at home with her mother, reading stories or helping with the housework.

Often the sisters would go out into the woods to gather berries, and if they ever saw a wild animal they did not run and hide, because all the creatures of the forest were their friends. The hare would eat cabbage leaves from their hands, the deer nibbled the grass all around them and the birds sang merrily wherever they went.

Sometimes, if it grew dark before the sisters got home, they would lie on the moss under a tree and sleep until morning. For they feared nothing and no one, and their mother did not worry either, knowing they would always come home, safe and sound.

Once, after a night in the woods, Rose-red stretched and looked about her, and there, sitting close by, was a beautiful child in a shining

white robe. Rose-red nudged Snow-white awake, and the two sisters stared at the magical stranger, who smiled at them, before vanishing into the woods.

When the girls got up to go, they realized that they had fallen asleep right on the edge of a cliff and that if they had gone a few steps farther in the darkness, they would surely have fallen to their deaths.

"It was your guardian angel, watching over you," said their mother, when they got home and told her what they had seen. "He stopped you before you got to the edge of the precipice and watched over you both till daylight, to make sure you were safe."

Now Rose-red was always the first to rise, and every morning, when the roses were in bloom, she would run out into the garden, pick a flower from each bush and put them in a small pot by her mother's bed, so that she would wake to their beautiful smell.

By the time their mother was up, Snow-white would have polished the brass of the kettle till she could see her face in it, lit the fire and

put the water on to boil. And on a winter's evening, she would close the shutters, they would draw up by the fire and their mother would get down the big book of stories and read to them. Beside them, at their feet, lay a little cat and behind them, perched on a low beam, was

a white dove, with its head tucked under its wing.

One night, in the middle of a story, there came a loud knocking at the door. "Who can that be, so late at night?" said their mother, putting down her book. "Run to the door, Rose-red, for it must be some poor traveler seeking shelter."

The girl thought she saw the figure of a man, standing in the darkness, but when she opened the door wide she realized it was no such thing, but a gigantic bear poking his great, thick head through the gap. Rose-red screamed and shrank back in terror, the cat began to cry, the dove flapped its wings and Snow-white ran and hid under her mother's skirt.

"Don't be afraid," said the bear, in a kindly voice. "It's freezing out here in the snow, and I only want to warm myself a little."

"Come in, bear," cried their mother, from inside the cottage. "Come in and join us by the fire. But watch you don't burn your beautiful fur." She called to her daughters to come out from their hiding. "I'm sure he's a good, honest bear and wouldn't dream of harming you. Fetch a brush, now, and beat the snow from his fur."

So the girls did as they were told. The cat and the dove drew near, too, and soon the bear was stretched out by the fire, purring like a great big lion.

In the morning he trotted over the snow back into the woods, and from that day on he would come to their door every night. The sisters grew used to the bear, and soon there was nothing they liked better than to tease him and tug him and ride around on his back.

Early one morning,
when it was spring and everything
was green again, the bear said to Snow-
white, "Now I must leave you, and I won't return
until the summer is over."

"But why?" asked the girl, sadly. "Where are you going?"

"I have to keep an eye on my treasure," said the bear.

Snow-white was surprised. "I didn't know you had any treasure."

"Oh, yes," replied the bear. "It's perfectly safe in the winter, when
all the sly little dwarfs are imprisoned under the cold, hard ground.
But in springtime, when the sun warms the earth, they break through
and get up to all sorts of mischief. That's why I have to go and keep
watch, for there's nothing they like better than gold and shiny things."

Snow-white was sorry to see her friend leave, but she opened the
door for him and as he went out he caught a piece of his fur in the

138

knocker. She thought she caught a glimpse of gold glittering beneath his hair, but she could not be sure.

One day, a little while later, the girls were out in the woods, collecting sticks, when Rose-red grabbed her sister by the arm. "What's that?" she said, pointing at a tree trunk in the distance.

Snow-white looked over and saw a funny little creature, jumping up and down. They crept closer and saw that it was a dwarf, with a bony face and a long, long beard. "What are you doing, little man?" asked Rose-red, giggling, for she was always the braver of the two.

"What do you think I'm doing, you stupid donkey?" hissed the red-eyed dwarf. "Come and help me!"

So they came closer still, until they could see the cause of all his jumping. "I was trying to split this tree trunk with my ax, but the hole went and closed up again before I could pull my beard free. Now I'm stuck fast, and all the two of you can do is laugh!" For the sisters found the sight of the poor little dwarf, jumping up and down in his rage, the funniest thing they had seen in ages.

"We're sorry," they said, trying to stop giggling, as they ran forward to help him. They tugged on his beard with all their might, but it would not budge. "There's nothing for it but to snip a bit off," said

Snow-white, pulling a pair of scissors out of her pocket and lopping off the end of his beard.

"No!" cried the dwarf at the sight of the scissors, but it was too late — the deed was done. "Curse you both, for chopping off half my pride and joy!" he raged, and he grabbed a bag of gold that he had hidden in the roots of the tree, swung it over his back and off he stomped.

A few days later, the girls went down to the river to catch some fish for their supper. As they came closer, they saw something that looked like a giant grasshopper, springing toward the water. And when they came closer still, they saw that it was the same old dwarf again.

"Going for a swim?" asked Rose-red, smiling.

"Of course not!" the little man shouted. "That cursed fish is pulling me in!" And there, at the end of the line, was a mighty fish, powering through the water.

They both took hold of the dwarf, to stop him from being dragged in, for dwarfs are creatures of the underground and water is the one thing they hate the most. "I was sitting here fishing," he gasped, as they fought to save him, "when a sudden gust of wind caught my beard and tangled it up in my line. Before I was able to free it, this big bruiser of a fish grabbed the line and started hauling me in!"

So the girls were pulling from one end and the fish was pulling from the other, and it must have been a monster of a fish, because even with Snow-white and Rose-red hanging on to him, the dwarf was edging closer and closer to the water's edge.

"There's nothing for it but to

chop at his beard," whispered Snow-white to her sister, and she whipped out her scissors and snipped away.

"Not again!" yelled the dwarf, his hand flying to his chin once he had picked himself up off the ground. "You were supposed to untangle the thing, not lop it off, you silly toadstools! How am I supposed to show my face underground with nothing but a stubby bit of whisker?"

So saying, he fetched a sack full of pearls that lay among the rushes and off he stomped with it, into the forest.

"Well, he's the most ungrateful man I've ever met!" cried Snow-white. "Twice we've saved his skin, and twice he's done nothing but shout at us!"

A little while later, their mother asked them to go into town to buy needles and thread, laces and ribbons. The road led them through rough ground, where great rocks lay scattered all about.

They were trudging along when they saw a mighty bird hovering above them. It was moving in slow circles, around and around, and then it dropped to a rock, quite close by. Suddenly they heard a sharp piercing cry, and when they ran forward they saw that the eagle had pounced on the same old dwarf and was about to carry him off.

"Help! Help!" screamed the little fellow, so the sisters seized him by the legs, refusing to let go. The bird had not the strength to lift all three of them into the air, and at last it gave up.

"You've torn my breeches to shreds, you careless hussies!" complained the dwarf, not even thinking to thank them. Then he grabbed a bag of precious stones and vanished under the rocks into his cave.

The girls were used to him and his ways by now, so off they went, into town. On the return journey, passing over the rough and rocky ground, they spied him once more, counting out his diamonds, emeralds and rubies. The evening sun shone on the glittering stones, and they gleamed so beautifully that the sisters stood and gazed.

"What are you standing there with your mouths open for?" the rude little dwarf called out. "Are you trying to catch flies?"

He piled his treasures back into his bag, and he was about to scuttle off to his cave, when a great bear trotted out of the woods.

"Help!" squeaked the little fellow, grabbing his bag and running the other way. But he was no match for the great, hairy beast. "Spare me! Spare me, and I'll give you some of my treasures!"

"YOUR treasures?" growled the bear. "Who says they're YOUR treasures?" For, of course, though the sisters did not recognize him at first, it was the very same bear that used to come into Snow-white and Rose-red's cottage every night, and the treasures that the dwarf had were the ones the bear had gone off to guard.

"Spare me and you can have them all!" promised the dwarf. "Spare me and gobble up these two plump girls instead!" And he pointed at the two sisters.

But, just as he did so, the bear whacked him with his paw, and he never moved again.

The girls had run off, terrified, but the bear called after them, "Snow-white and Rose-red. It's me, your friend!" They recognized his voice then, and stood still. The bear loped over to them and, as he

came closer, his fur fell to the ground and a handsome young man stood beside them, all dressed in cloth of gold.

"I am a king's son," he told them, "and I was doomed by that evil little man who stole my treasure, to roam the woods as a bear until his death should set me free."

Well, Snow-white fell in love with him, there and then. In time they were married, and Rose-red met his brother at the wedding and they ended up getting married, too.

The dwarf's treasure was divided up between them, they all lived together in a distant palace for many a long year and the mother of the two girls spent the rest of her life there with them. She brought the two rose trees with her, and every year they bore the finest red and white blooms.

Ali Baba and the Forty Thieves

In a town in Persia lived two brothers, one named Kassim and the other Ali Baba. Kassim married a rich wife and became a wealthy merchant, whereas Ali Baba married a woman as poor as himself and made his living by cutting wood and bringing it into town to sell.

One day, when Ali Baba was deep in the forest, he saw a troop of horsemen riding toward him. They had an evil look about them so he climbed a tree to hide, and watched as all forty men got down from their horses, pulled off their saddlebags full of loot and marched straight up to a steep wall of rock.

"Open, sesame!" cried the captain and, much to Ali Baba's astonishment, a door swung open in the rock, and the men walked through, before commanding it to close behind them.

The poor woodsman did not know what to think, but he stayed up in the tree, for he knew it was the safest place to be. After a while the door opened again and the robbers came out. "Shut, sesame!" cried the

captain, the door closed, they
mounted their horses and off they
went, to rob some more innocent travelers.

Once they were out of sight, Ali Baba climbed
down from his hiding place and went over to the rock,
to see if the same trick would work for him.

"Open, sesame!" he cried and, much to his delight, the
door swung open.

In he went, leading his three donkeys behind him, and found
himself in a magnificent cave. The only light came from a hole,
high above him, but it was enough to see that the place was full of
all sorts of treasures — rubies and diamonds, gold and silver. More
wealth than he had ever dreamed of.

"I'm rich!" cried the poor woodcutter, loading up his beasts with as many bags of gold as they could carry, not forgetting to close the door with a "Shut, sesame!" on the way out.

He covered the bags with sticks, so no one might suspect what was beneath, and when he arrived home his wife was overjoyed. "You wonderful man!" she cried, sinking her hands deep into one of the bags and letting the gold trickle through her fingers. "Let's empty them out and see how wealthy we are!"

But Ali Baba said, "It would take too long to count. Someone might come in and see, and then what would we do? No, the best thing is to dig a hole and bury it."

"Yes, maybe you're right," agreed his wife. "But while you dig, I shall weigh one of the bags, just to get some idea how much is in it."

Off she ran to Kassim's house, for she had no measure of her own. Kassim's wife, though, was a clever woman and a nosy one too. She hid some suet in the bottom of the measure, so that when it was returned she could study it closely, and what did she find stuck in the suet but a tiny piece of gold.

"Husband, husband!" she shouted, when Kassim came home from his shop. "Look what our poor sister-in-law has been measuring!" And she held out the shiny gold for her husband to see.

"Ali Baba and his wife don't have enough gold to count, never mind measure!" cried Kassim. "I shall go over and find out what he's up to." So he went to see his younger brother and he would not rest until he had found out about the forty horsemen, the wonderful cave and the secret password.

Kassim was already rich, but he was a greedy man, so early the next morning, without telling his brother, he rode out to the forest with as many mules as he could find. With an "Open, sesame!" he entered the

cave, commanding

the door to close behind him.

Well, wasn't he excited with all the treasures
there before him! Going straight to the bags of gold, he
piled them up by the entrance, ready to load on to his mules, but
when he went to leave he found that in all his excitement he had
forgotten the magic words.

"Open, shamash!" he cried. "Open, soshoo!" But whatever he said,
the door stayed firmly shut. "Oh, why didn't I bring my brother along
with me?" he moaned.

Sitting there, with his head in his hands, he wondered how he was ever going to get out when, at that moment, as if things were not bad enough, the door swung open and there stood the forty horsemen.

"What's all this?" roared the captain. "Someone is stealing our gold!" And with that, the villains drew their swords and rushed toward poor Kassim. They ran him through and hung his body from a rock, as a warning to anyone else who might dare to enter.

It was Ali Baba who found him, for he went to the cave later in the day and was horrified to discover the fate of his poor unfortunate brother. He wrapped the body in a cloth and carried it home on the back of one of his donkeys, covering it over with wood as he had done before.

Then, because he did not want anyone to know how his brother had died, he paid an old cobbler to come to Kassim's house and stitch the body up. But, so that the cobbler would not know where he had been, Ali Baba tied a handkerchief over his eyes before leading him to the house.

After the funeral, in order to prevent people from gossiping about how rich he had become, Ali Baba took Kassim's unfortunate wife as his own. It was common, in that country, for a man to marry his brother's widow, just as it was common for them to have more than one wife, so Ali Baba moved into Kassim's house with his first wife.

Meanwhile, the robbers had returned to their cave. "The body has disappeared!" exclaimed the captain. "We must find out who has been here, before they return and steal our gold!"

He ordered one of the men to go into town at first light, to see if he could find out who had been in their cave. As he passed through the city gates, the robber noticed the cobbler, sitting in his usual place, for he was always the first of the stallholders to arrive.

"How can you see to mend shoes in this light," asked the robber, "for you are so old?"

"Oh, I have been doing this for so long," answered the cobbler, carrying on with his stitching, "that I could do it with my eyes closed. Indeed, only yesterday I sewed up a dead body, in a place with even less light than I have today."

"A dead body!" exclaimed the robber, delighted with his luck. "And where was this?"

"I cannot tell you," replied the cobbler. "For I was blindfolded."

The robber guessed that if he blindfolded him again and led him out into the street, then the old man might just be able to remember the turns he had taken. So he offered him a large piece of gold to try it and walked by the cobbler's side. His scheme worked, for the cobbler led him, slowly but surely, to Ali Baba's home.

"Yes, this is the house," he said. "I'm sure of it."

So the robber marked the door with chalk and returned to his comrades. But Morgiana, a slave-girl of Kassim's wife, happened to come out of the house soon after and, seeing the mark on the door and thinking it might mean some sort of mischief, proceeded to mark all the others in the street in the same way.

That evening, the robber and the captain came back into town, looking to do harm to whoever had been in their cave, but because of Morgiana's trick they could not find the right house. The robber was furious, and the captain kicked him all the way back to their camp for failing in his task.

The next day, another of the troop went to see the old cobbler and offered him a second piece of gold, if he would only try again. Again the man led the thief to Ali Baba's door, and again the thief marked the house, but this time with red chalk and this time he made only a

150

tiny mark, where he did not think it would be noticed.

But Morgiana was too clever for him. She found the sign and proceeded to mark the whole street in the same way, so that when the captain and his man came to take their revenge on Ali Baba, again they could not find the right house and again the captain cursed and swore and kicked the stupid robber all the way back to camp.

"Next time I will do it myself," he roared at his men. "For you lot are too useless to be called thieves!"

The following morning, he bribed the old cobbler, once more, to lead him to the house. Only this time the captain left no mark. No, this time he simply stood and studied it carefully, noting all the many ways in which it differed from the houses on either side, and when he was quite sure that there was no way he could mistake it, he returned to the camp.

Then he sent his men to buy twenty-one mules and forty-one giant oil jars. He ordered them to empty all but one of the jars and to climb inside, which was a slippery, smelly job, but the captain had a fierce temper on him, so they did as he said. Then he loaded the jars on to the mules, one on each side, except for the last mule, who carried the only remaining jar of oil, and set off for the town.

Arriving just before dark, he led his beasts through the streets till he came to the house, which he recognized instantly. "I am an oil merchant," he said, when Ali Baba came to the door. "Is there any chance of a bed for the night, for I can find nowhere else to stay?"

Ali Baba did not recognize the robber captain, who looked very different in the guise of a merchant. So he agreed, for he was a generous man and had always been willing to share whatever he had, however little. He told the man to lead his mules into the yard and went off to find Morgiana, to ask her to prepare a bed and supper for his guest.

While Ali Baba was doing this, the captain unloaded the jars, setting them in rows. "When you hear me throw a stone from the window, climb out and join me!" he whispered into each one, and then he went into the house, where Morgiana was ready to show him to his room.

A little while later, the slave-girl realized that she needed some oil for the morning. As it was too late to buy any, she thought she would take some from one of the jars in the yard. She went to the nearest, and her little oil pot clinked the side as she reached out to fill it.

"Is it time to come out?" whispered the man from inside, thinking it was the captain, tapping the jar with a stone.

"Not yet, but soon," answered Morgiana in a deep voice, for she was a quick-witted young woman. She had no idea why there was someone hidden in the jar but, sensing danger for her master, she went down the whole line, clinking each one as she passed.

"Is it time?" asked a voice from inside, on every occasion.

"Not yet, but soon," repeated Morgiana, until she came to the last jar, the only one that contained oil.

Convinced now that the household was in terrible danger, Morgiana fetched a giant kettle, filled it with oil from the final jar and went back into the house. She heated the oil to boiling point, returned to the yard, and poured a great dollop over the head of each of the robbers, killing each man instantly.

Then she went up to her room and watched from her window to see what might happen. It was not long before she heard a tinkling from the jars and, glancing over to the room where the oil merchant was supposed to be sleeping, she saw him tossing down pebbles.

Getting no response, the robber captain stole down to the yard to
see what was going on and was horrified to discover that every single
one of his men was dead. Furious at how things had turned out, he
stormed off, back to his cave, where he plotted revenge on Ali Baba
and all of his household.

A week later, under heavy disguise, the robber captain made his way
back into town and rented a warehouse, where he set up as a merchant
of silks and other finery. There he got to know Ali Baba's son, who
was also a merchant and had a warehouse nearby.

One evening, the son invited his new friend to eat at his father's
house, just as the captain had hoped. Arriving there with a dagger
under his robes, the evil man waited for his moment. But when they
sat down to eat, Morgiana, who was serving them, noticed that the
guest took no salt.

She watched him closely, then, for it was rare to refuse salt in that land. She knew that any guest who did so must either be a stranger to those parts or must be planning some terrible deed, for generosity is valued highly, and even the wickedest person could never kill a man once he had shared his salt.

Studying the guest's face as she passed him his food, she suddenly recognized the false oil merchant and was determined to prevent him from carrying out his evil plan. So when the meal was finished and Ali Baba, his son and their guest were smoking together, she offered to dance for them.

Now Morgiana was very beautiful, and famed for her dancing, so Ali Baba and his son clapped their hands in delight as out she came, with a tambourine in one hand and a dagger in the other. As she performed before the men, she pointed the weapon at the heart of each, as though it was part of the dance, and when she was finished she went from one to the other with her tambourine, as was the custom. Ali Baba and his son each put in a piece of gold, but while the robber captain was reaching out his hand to put in a coin, she plunged the dagger deep into his heart.

"No!" cried Ali Baba in horror, but Morgiana tore open the silk merchant's garment, and there, underneath, was a dagger, even longer and sharper than the one she had been carrying.

"This is the man who killed your brother!" Morgiana told Ali Baba. "He is the false oil merchant, he is the captain of the forty thieves, and he was just about to kill you, master!"

When Ali Baba got over his shock, he was full of praise for Morgiana's wisdom and bravery. He freed her from slavery, there and then, and his son, who admired her greatly, asked her to be his wife. And Morgiana was delighted to agree.

Sources for the Stories

The Twelve Dancing Princesses

This is a retelling of a tale collected by Jacob and Wilhelm Grimm and first published in English in 1823. The story is also sometimes known as *The Dancing Shoes* or *The Shoes that were Danced to Pieces*. The Grimm brothers were told their version by the Haxthausens, a family of storytellers, who originally heard it in Münster, Germany. The tale probably dates back to the seventeenth century but does not appear to be very widely distributed, for although over a hundred variations are found in central and northern Europe, it is hardly known in France and not found farther east than Russia.

The Girl who Became a Fish

Andrew Lang, whose books I discovered as a child and have loved ever since, included this tale in his *Orange Fairy Book* (1906). It is a Catalan story, from northern Spain, and Lang used a translation of a version found in *Cuentos Populars Catalans*, by Dr D. Francisco de S. Maspons y Labros (1885). Many folktales deal with creatures from the sea, drawn to live on land (such as *The Little Mermaid* by Hans Christian Andersen), whereas this story works the magic in reverse. It also includes the popular storytelling element of shape-shifting.

Hansel and Gretel

The Grimm brothers are believed to have been told this tale by Wilhelm's childhood friend, Dortchen Wild, whom he later married. It is similar, in many ways, to a story by Charles Perrault, *Le Petit Poucet* (*Little Thumb*, 1697), which also features children abandoned by their parents in the woods.

It was the Grimms who named the children Hansel and Gretel (earlier versions only refer to them as Little Brother and Little Sister), who turned the mother into a stepmother and who made the father a reluctant partner in the children's abandonment. This abandonment is not included in the opera *Hänsel and Gretel*, written by Engelbert Humperdinck in 1893, a work which may well have contributed to the continuing popularity of the story.

Cinderella

The earliest recorded version, the tale of *Yeh-hsien*, comes from China and was written down by Tuan Ch'eng-shih around the middle of the ninth century. The first-known European version is *Cat Cinderella* or *La Gatta Cenerentola* from Giambattista Basile's *Il Pentamerone*, written around 1634. The story became very popular in England after the publication in 1729 of Charles Perrault's *Histories, or Tales of Times Past with Morals* (a translation of his *Contes de ma Mère l'Oye*, 1697), and it is this version that I have used as the basis for my retelling. I included an Irish variant of the Cinderella story, *Fair, Brown and Trembling*, in my previous Barefoot collection, *Tales from Old Ireland*.

The Fool of the World and the Flying Ship

I have based my retelling of this ancient Ukrainian folktale on the version that Andrew Lang included in his *Yellow Fairy Book* (1894). It is one of the most popular folktales featuring a hero or fool being sent on a quest into unfamiliar territory, and being set seemingly impossible tasks. Versions have also been recorded in Norway, Scotland and Nova Scotia. Arthur Ransome retold the story in his collection *Old Peter's Russian Tales* (1916), and a picture book version of his retelling, illustrated by Uri Shulevitz, won the Caldecott Award in 1969.

Rumpelstiltskin

The story of Rumpelstiltskin is well known throughout Europe, and the earliest version can be traced to Johann Fischart's *Gargantua, Geshichtkitterung* — an adaptation of Book One of *Gargantua et Pantagruel* by François Rabelais — published in the late sixteenth century. The Grimm brothers collected four versions, which they combined into the story of Rumpelstiltskin as it is best known in English-speaking countries today. Some other names for the little man, in different versions, are Tom Tit Tot (English), Whuppity Stoorie (Scottish), Kinkach Martinko (Slav), Tarandando (Italian) and Ricdin-Ricdon (French).

The Sleeping Beauty

One of the earliest sources for this tale is believed to be *Perceforest*, an Arthurian romance first printed in 1528. *The Sleeping Beauty in the Wood* was the first story in Charles Perrault's collection of 1697. Perrault introduced the spindle, the fairy gifts and the curse of the overlooked guest. The Grimm brothers then included a gentler version, which they called *Little Briar-Rose*, in their first collection of 1812. It is this version which has become the most well known (although Perrault's title is more often used) and which I have adapted here.

The Jeweled Sea

I have adapted this story from the version in *The Jeweled Sea: A Book of Chinese Fairy Tales*, edited by Hartwell James (1906). The folktales of China are some of the earliest recorded. For example, Confucius (551–479 BC) is said to have chosen from three thousand folk songs for the *Shih Ching* or *Book of Odes*, and the Han government (third century BC) appointed officials to investigate and report on legends and stories heard in the marketplace, as a way of judging the mood of the people.

The Celestial Sisters

This story comes from the Native American Shawnee tribe. The Celestial Sisters represent the constellation of Corona Borealis, a small, incomplete circlet of stars that rises high into the northern sky in summer. These stars have been the object of many legends: for example, the ancient Greeks believed them to be the crown of jewels belonging to Ariadne (who helped guide Theseus through the Labyrinth), which Dionysus, the god of wine, hurled into the sky when she died.

The Magic Ball

This is a retelling of a story from Argentina, which Charles J. Finger included in his *Tales from Silver Lands* (1924), the first folklore collection to win the Newbery Medal. Finger, originally from England, spent many years in Central and South America, working, traveling and collecting stories. He eventually settled in Arkansas and wrote over thirty books, mostly for children.

Snow-white and Rose-red

This story was adapted by Wilhelm Grimm from *The Ungrateful Dwarf*, by another German storyteller, Caroline Stahl, who published it in a collection in 1818. The "animal bridegroom" theme is also seen in stories such as *Beauty and the Beast* and may stem from the Greek myth of Cupid and Psyche. The name Snow-White is also, of course, found in other tales, notably *Snow White and the Seven Dwarfs*.

Ali Baba and the Forty Thieves

This is one of the best known tales from *The Arabian Nights* or *The Thousand and One Nights*, a collection of folktales from Arabia, Persia, Egypt, India and other Eastern countries. In the early eighteenth century, Antoine Galland translated some of these stories into French, their popularity spread throughout Europe and *The Arabian Nights* is now one of the most widely translated books in the world. Galland used the fourteenth-century Syrian text, the oldest existing manuscript of the basic stories, and added additional tales told to him by a Maronite Christian (from the Middle East), including the stories of Aladdin and Ali Baba.

Barefoot Books
Celebrating Art and Story

At Barefoot Books, we celebrate art and story with books that open the hearts and minds of children from all walks of life, inspiring them to read deeper, search further, and explore their own creative gifts. Taking our inspiration from many different cultures, we focus on themes that encourage independence of spirit, enthusiasm for learning, and acceptance of other traditions. Thoughtfully prepared by writers, artists and storytellers from all over the world, our products combine the best of the present with the best of the past to educate our children as the caretakers of tomorrow.

www.barefootbooks.com